DAISY THE DONKEY

PART OF THE SECRET DEMON SERIES

First Published in Great Britain 2022 by Mirador Publishing

First edition: 2022

A copy of this work is available through the British Library.

ISBN: 978-1-913833-18-3

Mirador Publishing
10 Greenbrook Terrace
Taunton
Somerset
TA1 1UT

Daisy the Donkey

Part of the Secret Demon Series

C. L. Ryan

www.angelicalskies.com

ALSO BY THE AUTHOR

Secret Demon 1

Secret Demon 2

Secret Demon 3

TABLE OF CONTENTS

Chapter 1

A new life

WITH A GENTLE PUSH I emerged into the real world, leaving my sanctum of warmth and protection to unceremoniously land with a bump onto the soft floor. Loving and encouraging words from my mother filled my head, as she tenderly licked the mucus away from my nose and mouth, urging me to breathe. I gasped, taking my first breath of crisp morning air deep into my lungs, coughing and spluttering, as I acclimatised to being outside my mother's body for the first time. For eleven long, warm, comfortable months, I had lived inside her, listening to her wise words of love and advice as she prepared me for this very day. Finally, I was born, there, alive.

"Get up! Get up and feed," she told me, again nudging me to move.

I opened my eyes; a strange two-legged creature towered over me, rubbing my wet glistening coat with something it's holding. Gentle loving words flowed from its mouth. I felt safe. I tried to get up, but my wobbly legs didn't feel like they were a part of me, and refused to cooperate. I started to panic, snorting little short puffs from my soggy nostrils. The fight for survival had just kicked in, and I needed to get up, I told myself.

"Come on, little one, you can do it!" my mother encouraged and called to me. I could smell her milk and was really thirsty. "Come and drink!" she whickered again.

With a jolt I was up and with the two-legged creature's help I wobbled towards her udder, which was now trickling with milk. I managed to reach it without falling over, grabbed the teat and instantly warm, sweet, life-giving liquid poured down my throat, and I swallowed it greedily. It had the desired effect and I could feel my body starting to come alive.

"Well done, little one," I heard the two-legged creature quietly say, as it stood back and watched me feed with a smile on its face.

Whilst mother gently nuzzled me with love, she told me that the creature was called a man and was there to help. My mother beamed with pride at the beautiful female foal beside her, delivered safely, ready for her new life.

"Well done, Blossom," the man said, "I think we'll call her Daisy. She's as pretty as one," he exclaimed, smiling as he left the stable leaving us to bond. And so I was named, my mother explaining to me that a daisy was a pretty flower that I would soon see.

I lay close to my mother that first night, cuddling into her warm furry body, not knowing what to expect, and falling asleep to her quiet words of love and pride which were filling my ears like a lullaby, singing me into a deep, deep, sleep.

The next morning was warm; the yellow thing in the sky my mother had told me was called the sun was shining through the stable door. Warm winds sent enticing smells drifting inside. My mother explained that it was called grass and that when I was older I would love its taste. She was hungry, and whickered through the top door to be let out. I was strong, bright eyed and feeding well.

"Not too much, greedy!" my mother said to me as I fed at her teats, pulling the sweet sticky liquid from her body. "Now then, stay with me," she ordered as the stable door opened and a small, dark haired, two-legged creature known as a woman entered.

"WELL DONE, BLOSSOM, YOU CLEVER girl," she said to my mother whilst scratching her under the chin and giving her what I later learned was a piece of juicy apple, to eat. "And welcome, Daisy," she said to me, gently placing something around my head.

"It's all right, little one, it's called a halter, we all wear them, there's nothing to fear," my mother reassured me, encouraging me to stand still and accept this new headwear, which of course I did. The woman then attached something to my mother's halter. "Stay close to me," my mother again called as we both walked out of the stable into the bright morning sun, towards where a young two-legged woman – a girl, my mother told me – was holding something open for us to pass through. All the time we were walking my mother was pointing things out and telling me what they were called. We were apparently in a yard and about to pass through a large white wooden gate.

"Oh, she's lovely, Mum!" I hear the girl say, as she reached out and touched me as I skittishly passed, my mother giggling at the sight.

"It's all right, they won't hurt you," she told me.

We emerged into what my mother said was a massive field full of lush green grass swaying in the breeze, and bursting with the colours of wild flowers and butterflies, which dangled awkwardly in the air, trying to visit as many flowers as possible in the breeze. It was a multicoloured canvas appearing in front of my eyes. There were other donkeys like my mother in the field and they all whickered with greetings before walking over to her.

"Well done, Blossom, boy or girl?" they called out as they approached us.

"Girl!" she replied proudly, now nuzzling and nudging me to walk forward so they could all admire the new arrival.

"Oh – lovely, beautiful markings!" they all commented, inspecting my tiny frame, oversized fluffy ears and dark stripy markings, which to a donkey were quite alluring.

We spent the rest of the summer in that glorious field, my mother and I, being together, gathering with the other donkeys, moving around as a family, helping and supporting one another with the youngsters when they got into mischief, as I often did. There were six new foals: me, Comet, Star, Lilly, Apple and Jessie. We would have races around the field to see who was fastest, and I always won.

"Let someone else win for a change," my mother would say to me, but I couldn't, I was faster and stronger than them all, and had a spirit within me to win, and I made sure I always did. It was a special gift that was given to me to help me survive, and I would never let it go.

My mother eventually had to go back to work; her rest after giving birth to me had sadly come to an end.

"Why can't I come with you?" I would always ask, whickering as loud as possible to her as she pulled the cart out through the cottage gate, and out of sight. She would return at the end of the day, tired and dusty, and would come and kiss me before rolling in the dust pit, and tucking into her welcome hay net.

Chapter 2

Separation from my mother

IT WAS A STRANGE SENSATION the day the six of us were put into another field away from our mothers. We called out loud to them, continually talking to them over the field fence, but we were never allowed contact with them again. For the first couple of months we were all heartbroken, huddling around the entrance of the field gate, just in case someone should come along and open it and take us all to them, but they never did. We would often see and hear glimpses of them as the cart passed the large hedges of the field, and we would run as fast as we all could to try and catch up with them. But they were bigger, stronger and much, much quicker than us, and would soon disappear out of sight and out of earshot.

When the cold nights of winter came, we six were put into a warm barn on the other side of the farm, with no contact now at all with our mothers, or any other animals. We all felt frightened, alone, and very, very lost. We should never have worried; we were all well fed and cared for. Every day someone would come and make sure we were safe and well, fill our water butt, fill our hay nets with fresh sweet hay, and give us a nice scratch under the chin with soft soothing words to reassure us we were safe.

Over the next year, our masters and mistresses would come every other day, and put funny leather halters on us with metal bars that went unceremoniously into our mouths. None of us liked this at first, but after lashings of sweet dark molasses were placed on the metal bit, we would stand quietly smiling as we sucked the sweet delicious sticky goo that trickled like nectar down our throats. Very soon we all agreed that the bits of metal in our mouths meant nothing and were now normal to us. Next came the saddle, a large leather seat with dangly leather straps with metal rings attached at the ends. As I was the largest of the donkeys, I was the first to have this placed on me. Steadily and slowly I accepted it until eventually one of the small children was able to get onto my back without me minding. She was actually riding me. I was attached to a long rein with the kind mistress, who was standing in the middle of the circle I was trotting in. Commands came to trot, canter, and walk. I obeyed instantly. I didn't mind, it was something new, but poor old Apple and Lilly really didn't like it, and no matter how the master and mistress persevered with them, they would not allow anyone to sit on their backs, bucking and braying out loud, most indignantly.

"Have to be driving donkeys!" the master shouted to the mistress one day after a long hard struggle with them both, neither one accepting the saddle.

"What a shame," the mistress replied, calming them.

They were both sweated up, foam on their flanks, and they were blowing hard with fear. They were rubbed down with soft bunches of straw, the master and mistress saying calming words to help them relax and comfort them. Jessie, Comet and Star on the other hand, like me, had no trouble accepting the saddle and the small riders on their backs, quite enjoying the experience and the attention it brought. It soon became obvious we four were now fine accepting the saddle and any rider on our backs. Training continued and we looked forward to the new arrivals at the farm every day. We would be tacked up and with small children on top, we would ride out into long leafy lanes, with the mistress in front of us all on her large pony Harry, and the master bringing up the rear on his lovely mare, Hilda. It became a regular thing, and the four of us loved it.

One particular day, it was very hot and the horseflies were really bothersome. They could give a nasty bite, and the four of us were quite vexed and skittish on the ride. We were all grateful to the master and the mistress for ending the ride a little earlier than expected, though the small riders would never know. After we got back, the children all left the yard happy and content with their ride, and our tack was removed, and big scratches were given to our backs, which itched with the attention of the horseflies. All haltered up, we were led back to our field as usual to be released and when the bridle came off, we were all free, and would run around the field, jumping and bucking, releasing our joints, ready for a nice roll in the dust pit. But first we would say hello to Lilly and Apple, who were always waiting for us, ready to join in on all the fun. But… not today! We suddenly realised after rolling around in the dust pit, that Lilly and Apple were nowhere to be seen. We all stopped in our tracks, nervously looking around for them, calling out their names as loud as we could, now horrified that our friends were not in the field. We all started running around the field again calling and calling for them, hoping for a response, but none ever came.

"Oh dear oh dear!" called out the kind mistress as she entered the field with a large bucket of chopped swede carrot and apple to help calm us, which of course eventually it did. Giving into the juicy morsels on offer after a tiring day, sort of made everything okay again. She rubbed our bitten backs, and said soft reassuring words to us as we ate the sweet temptation, not even realising that the knacker man had taken the two girls away only 10 minutes after we left the farm for the ride.

We missed our friends and the master and mistress realised this, and so to keep our minds and us busy, they started our cart training immediately. The training was long and at times exhausting but we all gathered in the barn every night nuzzling and reassuring each other we would be fine and safe, and of course we were.

One day, it was mine and Comet's turn to work, while the other two rested. We were both harnessed to the Sunday carts. Mine was bright red and slightly bigger than Comet's which was bright green. Both had soft tyres. These carts were special, and were only used for weddings, funerals and high masses, and today, it would be a high mass. It was Easter Sunday, a special event in the Catholic Church's calendar, and all the family from the farm would be attending the mass in the large village church of St Joseph, just outside Portaloo. My cart was first, driven by the master. I had three adults, and four large children aboard. Comet had three adults, and a small child aboard. With a double click of his tongue, we were off, the master guiding me, Comet following behind. We set off at a nice gentle trot pace, all the way to the church. The journey took 2 hours and all along the route we received admiring glances from those we passed. On arrival we were tethered in a long line outside the church, with all the other donkeys, ponies and carts.

Reagan, the local blacksmith was in attendance. He always came when a special mass was taking place. He would attend the donkeys, ponies and horses that needed an odd shoe which they had thrown, or he would be asked to look at certain animals if the owner thought they could be going lame; better than any vet was he. Walking down the street he stopped and admired me. He bent down and picked up my feet, and then he opened my mouth and examined my teeth.

"Nice animal," he remarked to my master. "Is she for sale?" he asked him.

"Next month's sale," he replied.

Reagan nodded and tipped his hat, walking over to a pony whose owner was beckoning him to attend a lost shoe.

"I'll soon have that fixed," Reagan reassured him.

The master and his family brought us both water and a small hay net before leaving us to attend the Easter mass, returning 2 hours later, and checking that we were okay. They then followed the crowd up the street to the local pub, to gather with friends and family over a pint or two of the black stuff, an Irish whiskey or a glass of sherry, as was the usual ritual. The priests from the church scurried behind them not wishing to miss their free tipples after a long hard, drawn out service.

"I'll let her have her head," shouted the master to the mistress who was driving Comet and the smaller cart, sometime later as we made our way home again.

"Race you!" she shouted back laughing.

"You're on!" he shouted back, already amazed at how Comet was now shoulder to shoulder with me.

I felt a sudden slap on my rump, and a call to extend and quicken my pace. I looked over and saw that my friend Comet was just starting to pass me. His cart was slightly shorter in length, and he only had three adults and a small child on board. Gosh, he was flying, but I wasn't having any of that! I always won, and I quickly surged forward taking back the lead, extending my large gait and feeling the cart following with me.

"Wheeeeeeee," gasped the master out loud for all to hear in sheer surprise at my speed and strength, Comet now receding back into the distance. We arrived home some 5 minutes ahead of Comet and the following family.

"Wow! That's some girl!" shouted the mistress, as a weary Comet pulled in through the gate. "Should get a good price for her next month," she smiled to the master who nodded, rubbing my sweaty body down with a large wet cloth, cleaning my mouth, eyes and ears, and giving me a well-deserved scratch under the chin.

We were both released back into the field where Star and Jessie were waiting. It was good to have friends. They greeted us, and we rolled in the dust pit together. It was a sight to see for all, the master, mistress and the family laughing at the four donkeys all rolling in clouds of dust, then chasing each other around the field, and whickering with delight.

The next morning, we were all tethered in the yard, being groomed and having our feet picked out, ready for work that day with the carts. I heard a soft voice call, "Daisy? Daisy is that you, m'girl?" I knew that voice instinctively; it was Blossom my mother. She walked over to me and nuzzled me instantly, and tenderly said, "Well done, Daisy, the master and mistress adore you! You will do well."

"How are you, Mother?" I asked her back.

"Fine, fine, meet Findlay."

I looked down to see a little colt at her side, a small halter on his head, keeping right beside her, just like I did all those years ago.

"Oh, he's lovely."

"Move on!" called the mistress to Blossom and the little colt.

"I'll never forget you, Daisy," she called out as the mistress pushed them on into the massive multicoloured field at the end of the farm with the butterflies that I remembered so well. Tears rolled down my big donkey face. My mother, my beautiful mother who bore me and brought me into the world had just said goodbye. Why? Panic suddenly struck. I became agitated and started calling out to her.

"Shush now, girl," said the master patting me on the back and starting to harness me to the cart for the day's work and trying to distract me from my meeting with my mother. He needed to get me back on track as a hardworking, strong girl, which of course, as always I did. But that day I was a little sadder.

Chapter 3

New shoes

IT WAS A BUSY MORNING, everyone in the yard was up early, but it was unusually quiet. Myself, Jessie, Star and Comet were being groomed to perfection, with not a hair left out of place, our hooves were also polished with oil, and we were given new white halters to make us look really smart. Sad and quiet faces were all around making things feel eerie. A large lorry sat in the yard. We had seen it before, but had never really taken any notice of its comings and goings over the long months. None of us realised we were actually going into the lorry, or even to the sale. Why would we? But something had left me with a sense of unease for days. Why had my mother said goodbye?

The master and mistress had kept us busy working on the farm, pulling the carts and giving rides to the local children. The day before, the man we knew as Reagan had called; we had just finished working with the carts and were hot and sweaty.

"Very fit," my master would comment as he took our harnesses off and rubbed down our steaming sweaty bodies with a large damp cloth. "Hi, Reagan!" called the master as Reagan pulled into the farmyard with his new van and portable forge.

"How are you today, Brendan?" Reagan asked, holding out his hand in greeting and friendship.

In all of the time that had passed, I never knew my master's name was Brendan. It was really odd hearing it and realising that this lovely man who had trained me and looked after me was called Brendan.

"All four please!" Brendan said looking at us.

We were tethered up to the outside of the stables, patiently waiting to be released back into the field, and our lovely dust pit.

"Big girl in the sale?" Reagan asked him quietly, nodding towards me.

"Yes, good, strong, fast and very intelligent. I should get a good price for her," he replied.

"What about the others?" Reagan asked back.

"All really good; been a long time since we've had a really good bunch like this." "Well done," said Reagan. "I'll be bidding; could do with a good animal," he commented as he viewed the lovely tethered beasts, still eying me especially. "You won't go wrong with any of them, we've trained them well, and they are all willing!" Brendan stated with a confident smile.

"Where are the other two?" Reagan asked.

"Knacker man; couldn't accept the saddle. Shame really, hate sending them away, but if the temperament isn't right, no point in selling them, they'll have a horrible life, be abused and ill-treated, making their life a misery, I just can't do it," Brendan stated quietly and firmly. "So, all four new shoes!" he instructed Reagan. "Fine," replied Reagan as he set about rekindling his forge with huge bellows, blasting air into the side of it, and bringing the already smouldering fire back to life, spewing heat hot enough to mould and shape the four sets of shoes he needed to make that day for the lovely animals he worked with.

One by one he expertly cut, rasped and shaped all of our feet, whistling and talking to us all the while, working as quickly and as quietly as possible, trying not to worry us, and as usual, he was always thinking about the beautiful beasts in his care. Every single animal's feet were different, and over the years that he had trained with his father, he had seen them all, and we four were no different. Comet's feet were slightly splayed to the side, Jessie's feet were very small and tight round, whereas Star's and mine were what he would consider normal. Working quickly and diligently, within 4 hours, we all stood in nice new and very shiny shoes, all prancing with delight at the sight of our very smart feet.

I loved mine; they were very shiny and strong. At first we all agreed they were heavy, and they made a funny clip-clop sound on the cobbled yard which excited us. The master and mistress reassured us as they led us back to the gate of our lovely field, and the dust pit, that we would soon all get used to the sound.

"Race you!" I called, romping around the field in sheer heaven; the grip was amazing, I could run even faster. I whickered out loud with delight. "Come on, Comet!" I called to him as he followed me, my hooves digging deep into the soft earth giving me faster and bigger strides. I out distanced the others easily as they tried to keep up.

The master and mistress came into the field, calling us all with a large bucket of treats. "Whoaaaa!" they both called reaching out to slow us charging animals who were excited and quite joyous at the special attention we had received that day.

We trotted over to them, interested to see what was in the bucket which they had been shaking to gain our attention. This was intriguing, quite a few times in the past they had come into the field with the bucket and each time it had been full of delicious things to eat, but today we were haltered and led back into the big barn at the end of the farm, away from all the other animals, a quiet place, undisturbed by anyone or anything. We were placed inside with juicy hay nets to munch on, troughs of chopped carrots and swedes, and a large vat of rainwater to drink. We were in heaven, but what we didn't know was that the master and mistress were worried that we were so excited by our new shoes, that we might hurt ourselves. With the sale the next day that was the last thing they wanted. Calming us down was therefore their main concern.

"Their new shoes have made them a bit frisky, we can't afford for any of them to hurt themselves tonight, especially after Arthur," Brendan quietly said to his wife. Arthur was their old donkey who had had to be put down after injuring himself in similar circumstances. Once we started to relax and munch on the sweet treats, they finally left us.

We all agreed that we loved our shiny new shoes, and we now felt really special, and grown up. They made us all feel really good, and nuzzling each other that night in the low fading light, we bade goodnight, butterflies churning in our tummies, excited at the prospect of being let out into the lovely field to once again race each other the next day. Gradually and peacefully we all fell into a well-deserved sleep.

The next morning did not go as we expected. We were all lined up in the yard, were groomed, our coats combed, our heads washed, and our feet picked out. Then we all had new white head collars placed on us which made us all feel very smart indeed. We all chatted to one another as we stood tethered in line, being manicured to perfection.

I heard a call, it came from the field gate, and I recognised it at once. "Daisy!" it again came; it was my mother.

I whickered back in acknowledgement. "Mother!" I responded.

"Daisy I love you, be good for your new mistress," she called to me.

All of us reacted. "What new mistress?" we all whickered back, but before we could react and say any more, or ask any more questions, the mistress shooed my mother away from the gate, just in time as the back of the lorry was opened.

"Mother, Mother!"

Chapter 4

The sale

I CONTINUED TO CALL AND call, but to no avail, she was gone. I now realised that I was obviously going somewhere, but where? We were all now very distressed. The master and mistress came over and helped load us all into the back of the straw floored lorry, staying with us in the swaying vehicle until we reached our destination, which felt like a lifetime. They were saying soothing words, trying to calm us, rubbing our furry heads and noses, and feeding us little pieces of sweet carrot and apple. But I could not eat mine; I felt sick and I let them all fall out of the corner of my mouth. I suddenly realised that I was alone, and that the four of us would probably never see each other again. Shock took me, and sadness washed over me like a wave. I tried to remember my mother's words - "be brave, little one, be good for your new mistress". I had to be strong, fear was rising.

Suddenly a large, sparkly blue and gold being with large wings appeared in the corner of the lorry and waved at me. "All will be well, little one, fear not," he told me.

I looked around at the others as the back of the lorry's ramp was lowered. We were all wide-eyed with apprehension, but all I could see was a mass of people, and all I could hear was loud voices. The shrill of horses and the bleats of harassed sheep filled the air. We were led out into a mass of moving people, the likes of which we had never seen before; all I could see was pens full of different types of animals. We passed pigs snorting and screaming as they were pushed out into a ring and the smell of roasting flesh pervaded the air and was sickening. We passed large stalls where people gathered eating big pieces of bread filled with I don't know what, but whatever it was they were enjoying it immensely. Shouts and screams of pitiful animals filled the air. I felt faint, my legs started to wobble and fear engulfed me as I was pushed and prodded by my master as he led us through the crowd before eventually tying us all up in different pens. A young man painted something onto my back before vaulting into Comet's, Star's, and Jessie's pens and doing the same to them before disappearing as quickly as he had arrived.

We all stood and quietly looked at each other; we were totally traumatised. What on earth was happening to us all? Above each of our pens was a blackboard. I had no idea what the words said but I supposed they were about us. The noise of the crowd was growing louder, and in the distance we could hear a man's voice shouting 'sold! Sold! Sold!' Star reacted by bucking and rearing in his pen, panic flooding his body and mind. Where were our master and mistress to comfort us? I called and called, worrying about Star who was now foamy, wide-eyed and sweaty with distress. Some people came into our pens to handle Star and this momentarily comforted him. I was prodded, poked, and had my mouth forced open several times. I felt sick when I felt fingers running around my teeth, only to have my jaw shut unceremoniously, time after time. I called again but I was not being answered. We were all terrified, and were now calling out to each other trying to give comfort.

The large man who we knew was called Reagan, and who attended us at the farm, came over to the pens, and spoke gently to us, trying to supress the fear which showed in our eyes. He spoke kindly to me. "Hello, lovely girl," he said pulling my fluffy ears gently, and telling me he was buying me to use on his farm. Another smaller, ginger haired man passed, telling Reagan he would be bidding against him for me, as he gave me the once over. Then he nodded and smiled before suddenly disappearing back into the swelling crowd.

"Be off with you, she's mine, Michael!" Reagan called after him. It seemed like hours that all four of us were left in our pens, each and every one quietly shedding warm donkey tears, knowing our lives were about to change forever. It was goodbye to our lovely meadows where we lived, our lovely dust pit which always made us feel so good, our lovely master and mistress, and our beloved mothers who had brought us into the world. Fear spread through our worried bodies at what the day would bring for us all. Comet put his head over my stall, and we gently nuzzled, just like we used to with our mothers. It brought comfort to us both, just for the moment, two good friends trying to calm each other in the eye of the oncoming storm.

The crowds were now thinning; all the sheep, goats and pigs had been sold, and were starting to be taken away by their new owners. Small ponies, donkeys and horses started to leave their pens. I was lost, alone and fearful, when suddenly a gentle hand touched my shoulder and the voice of a lovely man spoke quietly in my ear. "Tell them all not to worry. My name is Tom, your brothers and sisters will have lovely new homes with new masters and mistresses who will adore them. I have come to take you home with me to work on my little farm, and to be a companion for my wonderful elderly mother Margaret. We don't have much but what we have we will share with you, and you will be much loved and treated well and my four children will adore you. Now tell the others not to fret or be frightened," and with that he was gone.

The sun had started to rise, it was now about seven in the morning, and the only animals left were the ones in and around our small gathering of pens. Jessie was led out first and within minutes we all heard 'eighteen guineas, sold!' Star was next, he tried to resist, digging his hooves in the soft mud, but the big man leading him gave him a sharp yank, and he dutifully followed. Comet nuzzled me over the bars, ears back, fearfully calling to me as he was finally led away. This time I heard 'twenty-five guineas, sold!' Then it was finally my turn. I looked at the large sweaty man as he came into my pen. My knees started to gently knock and I could no longer hold on to my bodily fluid, and it was released with sheer panic as I was fiercely pulled out of my pen. I reluctantly followed him to where the remaining crowd was standing. I was the last animal to be sold. I quickly scanned the people around me and acknowledged the sight of my master and mistress, but they simply looked away, almost as if ashamed. I saw the big man Reagan, and the small ginger haired man who he was bantering with, but nowhere could I see the tall dark haired man with the kind voice and eyes. The bidding started at ten guineas, and soon passed the twenty-five that had been paid for Comet. It suddenly stopped and wavered around the thirty guinea mark, eventually finishing at thirty-five, a fortune for a common hinny. I was taken back to my stall, where my friends were also now waiting. I whickered to them with delight. Jessie was just being led away by a family with two small children, screaming with delight, touching and rubbing their new prize. Jessie was relieved and whickered back 'goodbye'.

"Jessie's gone," the other two whickered out fearfully.

"Now stop it both of you, we will all be fine, the kind man told me so!" I said, firmly, but I was shaking inside, perturbed about who had bought me, and where I was going. I was trying to be strong for my worried friends who were looking at me, trying to feel better about their future, and what it would hold for them.

We were all now very thirsty, hungry and exhausted and very, very, distressed, but we had no need to be. Suddenly, a lovely woman and two small children came and led Comet away, the two children kissing and patting him as he walked, and the next person who walked towards our pen was the man I knew as Reagan. I took a deep breath, looking up into his eyes, guessing, waiting for him to undo my pen gate, but he stopped, looked at me longingly, and then turned and undid Star's pen gate.

"Hello, lad, my name is Reagan, and you are coming with me, so let's get you home and sorted," he said stroking Star's long furry ears as he led him away into the distance, leaving me all on my own.

I stood and hung my head in sheer despair and started to fret. I was worried that I had been forgotten, but suddenly I heard that magical, beautiful voice and wondered whether I was imagining it. Was it just in my head?

"Hello, lass," it said as the man from earlier laid a large shovel sized hand on my head, reassuring me that the voice had been real. "Time to take you home." He led me out of the pen towards a large old battered pig trailer.

"Be Jesus, Tom, she'll never get in. Christ, she must be all of 14 hands and more," said the smaller, dark haired man now gasping at the sight of me and my new master walking towards him.

"We'll be fine, don't worry, tie us both in, I'll stay with her. Steady though, Johnny, this is one precious girl!" he told him.

I quietly and confidently walked into the back of the battered old trailer, and the smaller man tied ropes all around us to keep us secure, and soon, with a little nudge, we were off, nice and slowly. My lovely new master, Tom stayed at my side in the pig trailer and I almost collapsed with relief. I loved this man already and I didn't know why, but all I did know was that truth and love spilled out of him like a river, making me calm and relieved. I was now quite excited to see where I was going and who was going to love me. He told me about his family, my new mistress, Margaret, his mother who would love me to death, his wife Patsy, and the demon that follows them. He reassured me that I was in no danger should I see it, and that I was never, ever to be afraid of it, and if it did confront me, to tell it in no uncertain terms to go away. Then he told me about his four beautiful children.

He also told me that tomorrow he was going away with Patsy to a place called Dublin, and that I would be left with my new mistress and the four children. His oldest son would drive me tomorrow, he had good soft driving hands, and Tom would instruct him to use the nice Sunday cart. They apparently had two carts, one blue and one green. The green one was the Sunday cart. It was very posh and only used on special occasions. It had soft tyres and would give his mother a lovely gentle ride into town to do the shopping.

"Yes, Master," I replied, now knowing he could speak to me in my mind.

He also reassured me once again that I was going to be loved and well looked after. I felt happy and relieved as we slowly wobbled up a long and stony lane and in through a cottage gate where an elderly lady was washing plates outside on the cobbles in a tin tub.

"Tom!" she called as she saw us slowly entering the small farm, and stood gasping with admiration, as my master unloaded me from the pig trailer, and took me straight to the field gate, where he tied me up and gave me water, a fresh hay net and a bucket of chopped sweet carrots and turnips. I was famished and greedily ate.

"Oh, you beautiful girl," said Margaret as she kissed the front of my face, as I stood relaxing, hunger and thirst satiated for the moment. "Oh, Tom, she's beautiful, really beautiful."

"Yes, she's a great girl, Mam. We were lucky, everyone was after her, the bidding was high, but she was the only one I wanted."

"Well, welcome, beauty." She again kissed my face and rubbed my furry ears. "What's her name?" she asked him.

"Daisy," he replied.

"Well, welcome, Daisy. Oh, Tom the children will love her."

"Are they awake yet?" Tom asked her.

"No," she replied, still cuddling me.

"Well, let them sleep on and I'll quickly grab something to eat. Me and Patsy are going up to Dublin today and Johnny's giving us a lift to the station."

"Okay, son," she replied.

"Tom!" came a call from a tall, lovely, green eyed, blonde lady standing in the cottage doorway. "Breakfast!" she called out loud.

"That's my lovely wife Patsy, never worry about her, or that bloody demon you may see hanging around."

"Okay, Master," I replied, now feeling very blessed that I had people who loved me, and made me feel safe. I had finished all the food in the bucket, and he untied me and opened the field gate.

"Off you go, girl," he said taking the lead rein off, and showing me the lush green grass that was all mine.

I immediately bucked and whickered with sheer joy and elation at my new home and paddock. I ran around and around the paddock; I was free again and very happy.

"Steady, girl!" my master called to me. I saw him smile, a real satisfied smile, and I knew he loved me, and he and his family would always be true to me. I decided right there and then that I would always look after them, and love and respect them, especially my new mistress, Margaret.

I stopped and tucked into the lush green grass, filling my belly as fast as I could.

"She'll be fine, Mam!" I heard my master say to my mistress as they turned and walked into the cottage to eat the breakfast that Patsy had cooked, and just for one fleeting moment, I thought of my mother and her new foal, Findlay, and my friends, Jessie, Comet and Star, and wondered if they had been as lucky as me. Although I did not know it, they were all finding good, loving, working homes, just as my mother and the winged being in the trailer had said we would.

I took no notice of the red car leaving with the pig trailer on the back; I was too busy tucking into beautiful, fresh, sweet grass. I saw my mistress, Margaret moving around the outside of the cottage. It was a beautiful, warm and quiet morning. I gazed at the small farmhouse cottage, with a pigsty on the side of it, and the large barn where my stable was, and the two carts placed outside. They were exactly as my master had told me; one was blue and one was green. The green cart was a lot bigger, and had long leather benches, and soft tyres, just like the one I used to pull for my old master and mistress. Across from the paddock was a large vegetable plot, and next to that a large field full with swaying wheat which would soon start to fill out. Piles of drying peat were placed at the edge of that field. It really was a lovely scene, and I was suddenly very grateful to have found such a lovely new home. Thank goodness! I sighed and started to fully relax and found a nice sandy piece of ground which would now become my dust pit. I was in donkey heaven and somebody above, I don't know who, was looking after me, and at that moment in time, I smiled to myself and thanked whoever it could be for my beautiful new life.

Chapter 5

Trips to town

THE CHILDREN CAME RUNNING AND screaming out of the cottage door, straight towards me in the paddock. Margaret was calling to them to hurry and do their chores so we could all go shopping. They were delighted to see and meet me, their new animal, cuddling and kissing me on the end of my nose. Master Tom was right, they were all adorable, and I loved them instantly. I also loved all the attention that Megan, Trixie, Shamus and Tinker, as I heard my mistress call them, gave me. Master Tom had already talked to me about them; he loved them with all his heart and I could understand why; love and trueness poured from them all. I was now a big part of a kind and loving family, and I felt right at home.

Looking at the large green Sunday cart which was parked near the barn door, I wondered if we were going out today although I'd heard Margaret say something about shopping. The children were called back into the cottage, so I lowered my head down to the lush grass and carried on eating. The early sun was warm on my back, and a cool breeze meandered through the tall grass. I looked up across the paddock into the blue sky, which was dotted with small fluffy clouds that were slowly making their way towards the rising sun in the distance. This was now my home, I thought, suddenly realising how lucky I was.

"Daisy!" came the call I was waiting for.

I whickered, "Coming!" in my own donkey language and briskly trotted over to the gate where the family were gathered waiting for me. Tinker quickly harnessed me to the large green Sunday cart, and I took the family and the cart into town. Tinker drove expertly, he had good, light, gentle hands, just like Master Tom told me he would, and I knew exactly what he wanted me to do. I could hear it in my head, he had the gift, the whisper gift, and I was a happy working girl. In no time at all it seemed, we reached the little town of Gory, and I was tied up outside a very large store, next to two other animals.

"Hello, I'm Daisy," I said to the donkey and pony which stood quiet and unattended, waiting for their owners to return.

"I'm Arkel," replied the little dark donkey.

"I'm Harry," said the small brown and white pony.

And that was it; I had made two friends, who I would acknowledge whenever we met in the future. Tinker and Shamus gave us all little pieces of carrot. I think they were very proud of me, constantly giving me attention, kissing my nose, and brushing my body. I relished all this attention as it made me feel wanted and loved. I decided I would work as hard as I could for them, especially my new mistress, Margaret. I suddenly saw her and the two small girls leave the store, laden with bulging bags, which were quickly and safely stored aboard by the boys. With everyone up top we moved off up the long main road, stopping outside a shop where the children were screaming with delight when packages of hot food were given to them; sausage and chips I heard my mistress call it. I could smell the food, it wafted all around us, and happy voices filled the air, and I stood contented as they delighted in their unctuous, exciting meal.

I could smell rain in the air; it was coming from the north. An unnatural darkness crept in and around the little village, making me shiver, and I sensed something or someone near us. It crept up from behind and gave a foreboding feel to that moment, which Margaret reacted to.

"Tinker, have you finished?" she asked him.

"Yes, Gran," came the reply.

"Right, then turn us around and get us home," she instructed him, which of course he duly did.

We were off again, back up the hill that led out of town. I had to push into a good trot to pull them all and the heavy cart back up that hill. Tinker knew what I was doing, and he let me have my head and push on. I found it easy, and we were in a good pace now on the long road, I'd soon have them all home safe and sound. Tinker's light touch let me work without hindrance. He just talked to me soothingly in my head, and I now knew where I was going, and the long stony lane soon came into view. Master Tom had told me, 'always be careful in this lane, and pick your way through slowly to give a safe and comfortable ride'. I remembered his words as I steadily placed the cart in the right position to turn into the gate, stopping right outside the cottage door.

"Put her in the stable, boys," my mistress told them, as she and the two girls went into the cottage. Tinker and Shamus unhitched me, lovingly rubbing my sweaty body with straw. Then they put away the Sunday cart, and walked me to my new stable, with its thick bed of dry warm straw. A hay net was bursting with sweet meadow hay and a large vat of spring water was waiting for me. I was in heaven. The storm was creeping upon us and we all heard a dog howling in the distance.

"Better lock the door tonight," Tinker said to Shamus, as they said goodnight, both kissing me on the nose, and thanking me for all my hard work today, before quietly locking the door as they left. It was a blowy stormy night, and I could hear the demon scratching on the outside of the cottage, but the master had told me not to worry about him, so I didn't.

The next morning, it was bright and sunny. Margaret came out early, hearing me calling to her.

"All right, all right, lass I can hear you, I'm coming!" she called out to me as she walked over to my stable and unlocked the door. "There you are, m'girl!" she said with a smile rubbing my face with love, and walking with me to the field gate which she opened. She laughed out loud as I sped around the field whickering with delight. "You've work to do again today, Daisy, we're off to mass!" she shouted at me as I rolled with delight in my little dusty patch, before she went back inside to make breakfast and wake the tired children.

We once again set out for Gory, and my mistress was panicking as they were running late. They had to be at mass for 11am I heard her tell them, and once again Tinker let me go. I knew my pace; it's not too fast, but enough to keep the cart from pushing me, and I am was happy, settling in to my new life, working for my lovely family, and I loved pulling the cart. Very soon the little town came into view, and we went slowly down the hill towards the church, but there was no room to tie me up, so we headed for the pub down the road, which made my mistress very agitated. She shouted at the boys to tie me up quickly and follow her and the two girls. I saw her running up the road, holding her long skirts as she ran. Once Tinker and Shamus had finished tying me up, and getting me settled with hay and water, they were off. It was a quick kiss on the nose and they were gone. I spotted Harry further down the line. We acknowledged each other and settled in to munch on our sweet hay. We looked around and were sad to see that hardly any other donkeys or horses had been left with anything to eat or drink.

Oh how lucky are we? I thought.

A long time later, the family finally emerged from church. I whickered with excitement and did my little dance on the spot, just to show them how excited I was they were back. My mistress instructed Tinker to get us all back home quickly; they sky had changed and a menacing dark presence swirled all around the small village, the hairs on the back of my neck stood up in response. I felt fear and panic rising in my mistress, and when Tinker turned the cart around, and gave me the instruction to push on, I did, with all my strength, pulling up the steep hill out of the village and onto the long road which led home. I got so excited that I had to be pulled back a tad, but it did not hinder our progress. The nasty black storm was threatening and rushed to chase us home, the winged beings were all around us. I felt some danger, and pushed on. I knew it was the demon, the nasty one, I could sense him, and the skies were engulfing, trying to choke us with evil venom. I made it to the stony lane, and the cart wobbled angrily behind, but I had done this yesterday, and I knew exactly where to place it, as I rushed through the gate to stop right outside the front door of the cottage.

"Quickly, quickly!" the mistress called Megan and Trixie, once again instructing the boys to lock me in the stable. I did not mind, I knew trouble was looming, and could see the demon up in the large oak tree behind the cottage.

"I'm not afraid of you, demon!" I called to him as I was being led away to the stable.

"You should be, animal!"

"Tish! I am not!" I replied, hearing his horrible scream fill the air, making the two boys shudder and work even faster, putting me in the stable and the cart away safely before running back to the cottage to bed in for the nasty night ahead.

Thunder filled the air. Lightning flashed and lit up my stable all night. The wind swirled, and the rain pounded the roof of my home, and it was as if God himself was banging on the cottage door. I felt no fear. Master Tom had told me I would always be safe, but my mind was on my mistress and the children in the cottage. I sensed the demon outside and could feel his frustration as it exploded into rage. Sleep came later as I lay in my thick straw bed, now oblivious to the war raging outside.

No one came early to let me out and I called and called, frantic with worry and wanting to know that my little family were safe.

"Daisy!" I heard my name called, eventually.

I called back with relief; it was Master Tom and his wife Patsy. They let me out of the stable and I instantly went to my lovely field. As I fed I looked back over at the cottage and saw that the outside of it was badly burnt and scratched. Master Tom and Patsy were calling through the windows and banging on the door, when suddenly the door opened, and Mistress Margaret and the children emerged safe and sound.

"Thank goodness," I whickered and carried on munching, loving hearing the sounds of the family bonding. I then briefly caught a glimpse of that nasty demon hiding up in the oak tree.

The children once again came into the field with sweet pieces of apple and carrot for me, and I watched Master Tom and the two boys repaint the outside of the cottage where the demon had tried to get in. Watching this lovely family, I felt my heart swell with pride, all of them working together, loving each other's company, chatting and singing merrily as they worked. *What did that demon want with this kind and devoted family?* I asked myself. Perhaps I would never know, but I was sure that they knew the reason. It wasn't until little Megan looked into my eyes, and I in hers, that I realised she was very special. There was a second life that moved within her, shadowed by her big green eyes. *She's the special one,* I decided there and then, watching one of those large winged angelical beings wander around the yard, keeping an eye on her and the family.

Trixie too had the gift, but it was definitely more prominent in Megan. I also sensed something around Master Tom's wife, but it made me shiver. I didn't want her to touch me, she was somehow different again. I didn't like the dark light that surrounded her. I sensed it was a demon light, and when the family left some days later Mistress Margaret cried into my neck watching them leave through the gate to go to the station on their way home.

I had been bought to love and serve them all, but I suddenly realised that I was all the mistress had left; no one else would be around but me. She was lonely, her little cottage was miles from town with hardly anyone passing by on a regular basis, and so I would try and keep her company. I would always follow her around the field and yard and listen to her singing and chatting to herself. I would also always watch with interest the winged beings that constantly seemed to be in residence. But I was safe, and so was she. We settled into a lovely little routine of shopping once a week and just being there for each other. Our little journey of life together had just begun and it suited me fine, well for the moment anyway.

Chapter 6

Trouble in Ireland

BEEP! BEEP! CAME THE ADVANCE sound of the horn of the red car. I quickly got up from the grassy ground at the gate, which had been my bed for the night, and I whickered excitedly. "Master Tom, oh it's Master Tom!" I could hear him calling my mistress, he was fraught with worry, and concern echoed in his voice.

"Mam! Mam!" I heard him calling again and again, until my mistress appeared groggily at the cottage door, hardly able to walk.

Worried voices bounced around the little yard. Tom waved goodbye to the kind man in the red car and walked over to me, acknowledging my calls of excitement at having him back at the farm. I was very happy to see him, but also worried about what was happening inside the cottage. I did my little dance on the spot for him, as I always do when I am excited, and my reward was a warm juicy apple straight from his pocket.

"Now, Daisy, Mam's not well, we've work to do here today, girl, okay?" he asked me.

I nodded. "Work, the cart, oh heaven, let's go now. Let's go!" I whickered excitedly, stamping my feet in anticipation.

"No, not for a moment, I've other things to see to, your stable for one. I've also got to see to the pig and the other animals," he said rubbing my ears with love.

I watched in anticipation as he came back out of the cottage and started his chores. I always knew where he was, I could hear him whistling his Irish ditty. I was still standing by the gate, excitement filling me. I saw him go back into the cottage, and come out again, heading towards me, with a shopping bag and a list.

"Oh! My turn, it must be my turn," I excitedly said to myself. Master Tom went straight to the barn and pulled out the Sunday cart, along with my lovely harness and driving reins. I stood at the gate shaking; it had been ages since I worked on the cart. I felt like I had been in a prison shackled to my field for the last month. I loved to work, I always worked, and here I was about to work again. "Yippee!" I whickered.

Master Tom put my halter on and opened the gate to lead me to the cart. "Oh feck! Oh bloody hell, Mam," my master cried out in despair on examining my hooves. I had lost all but one of my shoes, and my other three hooves were badly overgrown and curved to one side, which actually made my feet uncomfortable. He tied me to the other side of the gate in the yard, and Master Tom returned from the stable with a hoof knife and rasp. He carefully removed the shoe that was left, and trimmed and shaped my hooves.

Gosh, just like the blacksmith, I thought, feeling relief that they had been cut. I was already more comfortable.

Once finished, I was quickly harnessed to the lovely Sunday cart. I loved pulling that cart, and we were off, his mind and gentle hands letting me have my head as we went down the stony lane, talking to me in his mind as we reached the long road that led all the way into town. I quickly got up speed, but oh what a funny sensation not hearing my hooves clip clop as I strode along the road. Instead it was a soft thudding rebounding noise. In fact it felt really odd, but I was working, and that was fine by me.

MASTER TOM CALLED AND SLOWED me, and we turned left into a long lush leafy lane. It felt a bit slippery, but I could see a small farm ahead, and the plume of smoke from the chimney rising high into the air meant people! We pulled up at the gate of the farm cottage where a large robust man worked at a hot forge, sparks flying up and away into the air as he struck the metal he was working on. My master called out that he was looking for a man called Reagan.

"Who's asking?" I heard the man reply.

"Tom Murphy," my master replied.

An excited Reagan stopped what he was doing and came to the gate, and shook my master's hand, pleased to see his old friend again. He then invited us into the yard. We were at the little farm for some time, the two men happily chatting away while Reagan the blacksmith worked on my feet. He put on four new shiny shoes, and I loved them! How happy they made me feel, just like a princess. They sparkled in the sunlight and I felt special and ready to work really hard for my master and my mistress. Happiness filled me, and I was now feeling really frisky. My master was back, I was pulling the shiny Sunday cart, and we were on our way to the shops in Gory.

We said goodbye, my master and Reagan shaking hands once again, promising to keep in touch and Reagan had promised to call in and see me and my mistress again very soon. Oh what a happy day!

As we pulled out of the leafy lane and back onto the long road, I whickered with delight, "Look everyone, look at my beautiful new shiny shoes." I trotted happily down the road holding my head up high with pride.

Master Tom slowed me again, and we pulled off to the right, down another long leafy lane. The trees here were high, their branches like massive umbrellas making it seem dark, but I knew where we were, it's the doctor's house, I had been there with my mistress only a month ago. My master jumped down and tied me to the tie post, where I would patiently wait while he was inside. The doctor opened the door and invited Master Tom inside. I found some shoots of dandelion at the bottom of the post. They were soft and sweet; I quickly nibbled them, savouring the sweetness on my tongue, just like sugar cubes, which I sometimes got from my mistress.

My master returned with paper sheets in his hands. He was fraught and angry. He turned me around, and gave me my head, pushing on up the lane until we reached the road. I tuned into him immediately. I knew exactly where I was, and pushed on, extending my stride. I loved going fast, my shoes gripping the road, and I was happy. I pushed into an extended trot; my fastest pace was a trot, almost cantering, but staying in extension we flew along the road. The wind was whistling through my ears, and I loved the sound of my shoes clipping and clopping on the road, my master letting me work.

Suddenly, from nowhere I heard a beautiful shrill call, calling to me. I looked around and saw a stallion racing me in the field I was trotting adjacent to. He's handsome and strong.

"Look over at me, join me," this handsome beast called to me as we raced. We were neck and neck. His field ran right next to the road. "Join me! Join me!" he called again, his beautiful chestnut coat glistening in the late afternoon sun.

My master loved him also, and he whistled to him, making him even more excited. He knew he's a picture in horse flesh. His eyes were wild and attractive, and my stomach tightened. I trotted higher now showing off how beautiful I was, and he knew it. I saw a lovely white star in the middle of his forehead. He was looking at me! He was looking at me! I panicked. "I must work, I must work," I told myself, pushing on even harder, trying to ignore the butterflies in my tummy. My master again whistled to him, which of course he loved, but the stallion's call was soon lost in the distance.

When we got to the edge of town we called into the catholic church before then going to the chemist. The next stop was *O'Reagan's*, the big store which my mistress loved so much, and then lastly the *Royal Oak*. After the last stop and with all the shopping gathered, we headed home, the warm gentle wind pushing in and around us. The sun was lowering in the sky, bringing low orange and grey blankets in the distance above the tall towering pines reaching for the heavens above.

Again, the shrill call came as we passed the stallion's field, and again, he was racing us. *Gosh he is handsome*, I thought to myself.

"Join me! Join me!" he called again and again. His long strides pulsed through the lush turf of his field. "I will find you, beauty!" he called as I pushed on to get my master home to Margaret and our lovely cottage.

Finally, puffing and blowing I pulled into the yard through the cottage gate. I knew exactly where to place the cart so everyone can go straight into the door once alighted. My mistress came over to me, cussing Tom, but I was very happy. I had worked today and felt frisky and well, loving the attention. I danced on the spot for Margaret to show her how happy I was, and to show off my shiny new shoes. She kissed and cuddled me, and as always, thanked me for my work. I loved to work, I loved her and Master Tom, and all of the family in fact, so they really didn't have to thank me, it's what I loved to do.

After a glorious rub down I was allowed back into the field. I rolled in the dust pit, my favourite place, and then watched as Master Tom filled hessian bags with my excrement. I was fascinated by why he was keeping it in the corner of the paddock, and why he was also putting some into a large vat of water, which he then sprinkled over the vegetable growing in the next field.

I followed him around, lovingly nudging him from behind as he worked into the balmy night just to remind him that I was there. A sudden change in the wind told me a storm was coming. I could smell rain in the air, coming from the east, and the strengthening wind was pushing the moist air towards us. I could sense the wheat in the adjoining field, as it waved its heavy seed laden heads in the growing wind, as flashes of lightning illuminated the distant sky.

Master Tom ran for the cottage as large button shaped blobs of rain fell, and thunder boomed in the distance, the sky an angry amber colour. I sheltered under a tree. The rain was heavy, but refreshing. I detected the ground sighing with relief, the moisture rejuvenating tired, dry earth; it had been weeks since it had rained.

I was near slumber; thunder and lightning never worried me, when suddenly, I was shaken by a shrill call, and the thundering of hooves through the soaked earth.

"I have found you, beauty," the stallion from earlier called to me, slowly approaching after jumping the large wall, his handsome coat glistening in the rain. The whites of his eyes were glaring towards me with a passion I had never known before. Excitement filled my belly and I stood, looking at that glorious beast, my heart racing. He snorts, searching for my scent.

"Yes, you have!" I replied.

As he approached, his eyes stayed focused on me. His nostrils were wide and snorting, and he gingerly and slowly stretched his neck out. We touched, nose to nose, and my own passion arose, and my tummy tingled. This beautiful beast aroused my interest, he smelled divine, a real masculine stallion odour, which is irresistible. We greeted one another, and gently played in the now drizzling rain, chasing each other around the field, nipping and nudging each other lovingly. We coupled, but I felt no pain, only love, and a tingle shot went through me, ripping my being apart. It faded and repaired. I felt his seed implant immediately.

"I will never leave you, beauty," he told me, gently.

"You will," I replied, "you have to, this is not your home."

We touched and pushed our bodies together all night, nuzzling each other lovingly until the bright morning sun brought the song of the skylarks and the call of the cockerel announcing a new day. We stood together in the corner of the field, fresh breezes cooling us, as our tired bodies steamed away the night's rain.

Master Tom emerged early that morning. "Oh, feck!" I heard him cry upon seeing the stallion.

I whickered, "It's okay, Master Tom, he's my friend."

"Daisy!" Master Tom called to me.

The stallion, whose name was Legend, now knew my name and called to me again. "Don't go." He was now stamping his front hooves in indignation. "You are mine!" he again told me, calling again and again.

"Oh silly you, he's my master, Tom is his name, and he's a good man," I told him as I gently walked towards Master Tom, feeling my belly already filling with his progeny.

Master Tom whispered words of love to me, as he rubbed my small love wounds with salve, worrying out loud about the beauty in the field that was snorting and prancing around, watching me being handled gently by my master. Master Tom skilfully caught my suitor, and brought him to the gate where we greeted one another again. Master Tom loved Legend, I know, he loved all animals, but Legend was beautiful, masculine and I had his offspring buried deep inside my belly. He settled beside me, and we nuzzled, whilst all the time Master Tom was talking to him, nursing his scratches and abrasions. They conversed for some time, and all the while he attended to us both while we were tied to the cottage gate.

A short while later two young men came running through the gate looking for my lover. Legend spied them and reacted angrily; snorting and pawing the ground, but Master Tom reassured him that he was safe.

Before they led him away, he turned and told me that I was

beautiful, and that he would never forget me. "I am the Legend! Your foal will be like me! Fast and furious on the long mile."

Master Tom instructed the young men on how to handle the beautiful horse they were holding. I took a long and lasting look at my companion, and as quickly and as suddenly as he had arrived, he was gone. Walking through Margaret's gate into the stony lane and back home to his stable, leaving me with memories of our night of passion. Something I had never before experienced, and the gift of a new life implanted in my belly, already alive! And kicking - literally!

I looked for Legend on the way to Gory as I took Master Tom and my mistress to mass the next morning, but he was not there. I could still hear his shrill calls of love as we trotted past his field, and I could hear Master Tom worrying about me, my foal, Margaret, and how she would cope. I knew all would be well, and trotted on towards town with my head held high. I also noticed an angel riding on the back of the Sunday cart, but the best thing about that day was my shiny new shoes!

As usual, I was tied up outside the church on the main road in the town. Harry the pony and Arkel the donkey were my companions that day, while our owners attended mass. Water and fresh hay was always left to keep us amused while our owners prayed. We watched them with interest and amusement as they passed us heading towards the *Royal Oak* once the mass had finished, no doubt relieving their thirst, and loving the company of their friends and neighbours.

I loved talking to Harry and Arkel, as it made me realise just how lucky I was to have Margaret as my mistress, as well as Master Tom, and the rest of the family who absolutely adored me. We would often talk quietly, hearing of other animals being starved or mistreated by their owners. You always knew when you saw them; the sadness in their eyes gave it all away. Some chose death over a cruel owner, such was the pain and misery they endured, but we three friends were happy, and very lucky, and stood contentedly, waiting to take our masters and mistress back to our loving homes, when they needed us to.

Unusually, that afternoon, Master Tom brought my mistress back to the cart, leaving her with me, while he leaped up the steps of the church to confront Monsignor Doyle. I had heard hard words about the monsignor, and it was really funny seeing all the congregation file out of the pub and follow Master Tom to the church. After much shouting and clapping of hands, Master Tom returned to the cart and my teary eyed mistress. He hopped into the cart, and with a double click of his tongue we were off, once again heading home, up the hill out of the town and turning left onto the long road that led home. I don't know what went on that day, but I sensed them both relaxing, my senses feeling through the reins, and again I was happy.

The smell of the countryside filled my nostrils, wild flowers and the smell of lush green grass filled the air, satiating my new and unusual maternal feelings. I loved this time of year. I relaxed as I trotted home feeling quite odd. A sort of calmness had come over me and I was happy and content. I thanked the angel who I knew was sat on the back of the cart, and suddenly without really knowing it, so lost was I in my thoughts, the stony lane came into view. We slowed and I picked my way up the lane, placing my master and mistress right outside the front door. A warm piece of juicy carrot and a lovely scratch under the chin was the reward from my mistress, which of course I always loved.

A good rub down by Master Tom followed by a nice gallop around the field and a roll in the dust pit, contented my inner being and I settled to greedily eat the lush green grass that waited for me. I watched as Master Tom dug the vegetable patch, and as usual I followed him around. I loved to nudge him; it was our game, to remind him I was there, there for all of them.

"Please just use me!" I would say to myself. It always made him smile, making him whistle even louder; we always knew where he was, his whistling gave him away, you could hear him hundreds of yards away. This was a comfort to me and my mistress knowing we were not alone. I watched fascinated as he sprinkled holy water all around the farm and even over me, before going to bed. It made me smile.

When the family came to visit, the nasty black and green monster would always appear and usually it would sit in the oak tree behind the cottage… Was this the being he was trying to protect us all from? Yes, I think it was, of that now I am sure, but the angels told me not to worry as that was why they were there, and they would protect us all. I thanked them, but it set a worry in my mind that I realised there and then, would never leave me.

Chapter 7

Birth

MY MISTRESS LOVED ME, I knew that, she told me every day. My belly was swollen and I could feel the new life inside me move and kick. It was an uncomfortable time, I was able to work, but I was feeling tired. My mistress understood and didn't ask too much of me, and I worked at a slightly slower pace, feeling my tummy sway with the heavy burden I carried. It was a worrying time for my mistress, and I felt a little apprehensive.

We arrived back after a lovely drive, my mistress fussing over me as usual. My back ached and my head was fuzzy. I stood and let her lull me into a secure and trusting dream, as she lovingly brushed me and cleaned my face, telling me my baby would be born soon, and she wanted me to look my best, as I would be the very first thing it would see. The strokes of the brush against my swollen girth calmed my lungs; they felt tight, and my breathing was slightly heavy and laboured, but I felt nothing but love all around me.

"There," said my mistress as she washed my face and tidied me, rubbing my belly with love and pride.

She had made up my stable; perhaps the time had come? My foal had gone quiet, and I felt full to burst. A candle flickered in a jam jar high above me on a shelf. There was fresh water and a lovely thick carpet of straw on the floor along with a full hay net and a bucket of chopped goodies waiting for me as I was put to bed. Margaret kissed me goodnight, and as I dived into the bucket, I heard gentle whispers from her as she closed and locked my door.

"It won't be long now."

I had suddenly felt the urge to eat and savoured the freshly prepared roots. I would need all my strength, of that I was sure. I was not wrong. Nightfall brought the usual silence I was used to, and that night muffled feathers gliding in the moonlight, a barn owl hunting on its usual path, and fuzzy, fluffy moths fluttering all around the jam jar with the candle, were my only company. The smell of food cooking in the cottage wafted all around, and I was in my lovely stable, tired, not sure how I felt and trying to sleep. All I knew was that I had an uncomfortable day, and now odd twinges were about me, and a new day was not far off.

A terrible pain ripped through my entire body, shaking me to the core, wobbling my very being. Sickness and fear engulfed me and I took a deep breath and sipped the cool water in the vat, and for the moment that calmed me. Again a savage pain flooded through me; my foal would be born soon, I knew.

An angel appeared in the corner of the stable, one I had seen before. He was smiling at me, nodding and gently telling me in his mind that, "All would be well!" Another pain, bad! Excruciating. It dropped me to my knees. I was gasping, trying to breathe. "Daisy, please get up, be brave," he again gently urged.

But I was trembling now. I felt sick and my head had started to spin. Pushes and pain confused and frightened me. I was overwhelmed with the unknown. The contortions ripped through my belly and my tongue pushed hard out of my mouth, bile ejecting from my stomach.

"Help!" I cried in anguish, unable to control what was happening to me and again and again pain shot through my tired and confused body, but I managed to get up. I took a deep breath. I was at this moment, stumbling around the stable, my panic and pain at its height. I was in another world, one I had never known, and certainly not mine, when suddenly I felt a pop from my rear end. Fluid released from my body, easing the pressure, and reducing the pain immediately. I could at last breathe easier. I let out a long sigh, and the angel in the corner approached me, and told me I was nearly there. My swollen belly went solid as he spoke, as another uncomfortable feeling hit me, and then the pain intensified. I could feel this new life leaving my body on its journey into its new world.

"Stay strong!" were the words resounding in my head.

I felt a massive push and I knew my foal was coming.

"Help me!" I cried despairingly.

"Daisy lass," was a voice that comforted me. Suddenly the stable door opened and in walked Reagan the blacksmith. "Oh God!" he stated, immediately helping me, grabbing my foal by its hind feet and pulling the beautiful new life out of its sanctum, and my exhausted body.

With one last massive push and pull, my foal was released from its cocoon, and flopped onto the soft straw. I turned to look and there he was my beautiful foal, born, brought into this world, and now free of my core. I loved him immediately, and suddenly realised and understood how my mother must have felt when I was born. He was the result of my beautiful night of passion, a wonder in the straw, wet and slimy and trying to stand, just like I did, and apart from Master Tom, my mistress and the family, he would probably be the only other family I would ever have.

My milk arrived right on cue, almost as if by magic, Mother Nature taking over where necessary to provide the needy infant with its all-essential first nourishment. I called to my little one to come and feed, and long wobbly legs stumbled around the stable as he tried to make his way towards me. My teats dripped with his life-sustaining nectar. Again and again I called and encouraged him to come and feed, and when we finally connected, the bond was sealed. I felt complete and content. The angel smiled at me and left, just as suddenly as he had appeared; his job was done, my foal was here, and a new life had begun.

My foal suckled, relieving me of my liquid burden, which had scrunched my bladder making life uncomfortable, but now, oh heaven! Hunger suddenly attacked me as my foal fed. His name was Dandy! I had heard Margaret and Reagan give him his name earlier. Satiated and very full, Dandy lay down to rest. His journey had been exhausting for us both, but hunger and tiredness distressed me. I needed attention, so I called to my mistress. I needed food. Reagan and my mistress came running, the sight of my lovely son sleeping quietly in the deep lush straw, brought tears to their eyes, and again I whickered to get their attention.

"Oh, my lovely girl, sorry! Food, Reagan!" she called to him.

The next morning little Dandy was up, strong and ready to come with me to the paddock. Again and again memories flooded into me, as I remembered my first time out with my mother. Life had turned full circle. Suddenly, in the back of my mind, the pain of being separated from my mother hit home, and I realised for the first time in my life this was real life! Images of my mother with her new life, and a new foal had upset me as she said goodbye, and now it all became so real as I ushered my own little foal towards the paddock.

"Stay close to me, little one," I told him as Margaret put his little halter on. I reassured him that I was also wearing one. He did a little dance on the spot, even relaxing around my mistress as she fussed around us.

The warm sun invited us into the paddock, where wild flowers poked their heads above the long grass that swayed in the breeze. Flying insects of all colours were scattered in all directions as Dandy excitedly galloped around the field in sheer joy.

Margaret stood watching in awe and wonder at the frolicking pair playing together, but the serious job of eating the lovely green grass was far too enticing to resist, and we soon settled into feeding, a routine that would be with us both for the rest of our lives!

Chapter 8

The wager

THE WEDDING WAS HUMMING ALONG quite nicely. The band could be heard playing softly in the background, and happy couples were shuffling around the dance floor, singing along with the band as other happy guests sat quietly chatting and finishing off their sumptuous wedding meal. Megan and Trixie were happily chatting to their grandmother Margaret in the marquee, all three sat at the table, nibbling leftover food, and watching everyone dance, oohing and ahhing at the sight of all the beautiful bridesmaids and their dresses being whirled around by their suitors on the cramped dance area.

Tom on the other hand was working hard behind the bar, pulling pint after pint, and scraping the foamy top off, before lining them up like rows of black and tans. There he left them to settle, resting the beloved Irish drink, treating them as the Irish would say 'as gently as a woman', and nurturing them to perfection before consumption.

Patrick McConnell spied Tom working away at the bar. He was the cousin of the groom and came from a large gypsy group based on the east coast of Ireland, mainly from Kilrush. He owned The General, a fabulous fifteen hand, brown and white piebald trotter, unbeaten in his last ten races.

"Tom!" he called as he walked towards him with his hand held out to shake Tom's. "That's a fine hinny you have, I hear she's quick," he said.

"Aye, good lass she is," Tom replied, not really looking at him while he was busy pouring Irish whiskey into small tot glasses for the thirsty revellers now lining the bar.

"Fancy a wager, Tom?" Patrick asked. "Prize two hundred guineas."

Tom was momentarily startled: two hundred guineas!

"Sorry, Patrick, I don't have that sort of money."

"Oh don't worry, Tom, just put her up. If you lose I take her, if you win, two hundred guineas are yours," he replied, a nasty grin forming on his ugly, wind-battered face.

"Can't risk that, Patrick, she's all Mother has. I can't afford to lose her over a silly bet," Tom replied, as he silently thought to himself, *Christ bastard*! He was angry at his insolence, Patrick knew they were a poor family, and that to lose Daisy would break Tom's mother's heart.

"Tom we'll have a wager then, fifty pounds each, winner takes all, what do you say?" He again pushed Tom to get his attention.

That's better, thought Tom, he could find fifty pounds.

"Tom!" Patrick again pushed him, agitation rising in this greedy man, who felt he would wipe Tom off the face of the earth with his General.

Tom continued to think, went quiet for a second, sucked in his breath, and then looking directly at this large man who stood in front of him said, "Okay, when and where?"

"Good man, Tom," Patrick replied with relief written all over his face, "the day before the May Day fayre, one hundred acre field, it'll be a racing festival. There's also an open. I hear you have another beast?" he asked him with a quiver of expectation in his voice.

"Maybe," Tom replied trying hard to hide his excitement, yet feeling sick at the same time.

"A deal then?" Patrick again asked feeling somewhat exasperated.

"Deal," agreed Tom. "I'll race Daisy, but I don't know about the other, I have to see what the competition is on the day."

They both spat on the palms of their hands and shook on the deal. The onlookers were amazed; Tom Murphy had just agreed to a deal, probably a race; his new hinny against The General.

"The General!" shouted a shocked Miller O'Brien a local stable boy. "He's no bloody chance against The General. Who's taking the book?" he shouted in a mocking tone so that everyone could hear. Heads turned in their direction and it suddenly all became real.

"I am," called a voice from the other end of the bar. It was Miles O'Leary the local bookie.

"Well I'll have fifty pounds on The General to win!" he shouted again, now waving a bundle of notes in the air for all to see.

"Christ shut it!" Tom shouted, and gave a glare for all to see.

The crowd were excitedly gathered around Miles, the book was already out, and bets were being placed. Reagan came running over to the bar after hearing all the uproar.

"Be Jesus, Tom, we're going to race Daisy? What about Dandy?" he ecstatically shouted loud enough for everyone to hear.

"For God's bloody sake, Reagan," replied Tom, pulling Reagan towards him and using the glare which always told you to be quiet.

"Who's Dandy?" called someone from the crowd gathered around the busy bookie.

"Sorry, Tom!" said Reagan sheepishly.

"Keep it quiet, Reagan, you don't know who you are dealing with here, there's always danger in every wager, especially if we win."

"Oh God, Tom what have I done? Do you think Daisy can beat The General?" he asked in a whisper, shaking at the thought of a race, a nervous sweat now breaking out on his forehead.

"I do, Reagan, I do, but it has to be planned, the feeding has to change, and we need to train them both," he replied with a very serious look on his face.

"Both! Oh God in heaven, Dandy will destroy them all he's so fast,"

Reagan again shouted out with sheer excitement. He was already seeing pound notes in front of his eyes and feeling the wad in his trouser pocket. His head was in a whirl as he imagined pots of gold stacked in his bedroom.

"Fucking hell, Reagan, shut it!"

"Sorry, Tom!" he replied, taking a hold of himself and his senses, and once again feeling silly and very sheepish.

"We'll speak before I leave and make a plan, okay?"

"Okay, okay, Tom," he heard himself say as he walked away trying not to draw any more attention to himself.

A large happy roar filled the air; the Southern Irish Dance Troupe had arrived and the focus, thank God, was switched to them, leaving the excited punters in a quiet corner of the bar making the book for the race day.

The day after the wedding there was much for Tom to do at the farm and so he was up and out of the cottage early. Reagan pulled up through the gate in his cart which was being pulled by Star, Daisy's brother. He was trying to be as quiet as possible so as not to wake Margaret and the two girls. Daisy let out a low whicker acknowledging her brother. A very quiet and confidential meeting took place behind the barn that morning, Reagan scribbling furiously all the instructions Tom was reciting to him. He left as quickly as he had come, leaving Tom working in the field, and Margaret and the girls not even aware of his visit.

The wedding had been a great success and a beautiful, happy day Margaret had remarked the next morning, thinking back again to her own wedding. She wore a lovely comfortable smile as she went about the breakfast. Tom was already hard at work and he had planned and planted the new crops that they would need as part of the training programme for Daisy and Dandy before he left.

"Tom, what in God's name are ye planting winter kale for, I'll never be able to eat all that?" asked Margaret now quite vexed.

"Mam, it's good fodder for the beasts, and now we have Dandy, it'll save money on hard food," he told her. Margaret accepted his comments for the moment, but was now worrying about how on earth she was going to get out into the field to harvest the bloody stuff. "Oh don't worry, I have already asked Reagan to call in and feed Daisy and Dandy, don't worry, Mam, it's all in hand," he told her, making her suddenly jump. It was as though he had been reading her thoughts.

And so it began with weekly letters arriving from Tom and Reagan taking the whole thing deadly serious and holding to his part of the bargain. Daisy and Dandy were kept working hard, Tom pushing Reagan to increase the length of work from one mile to one and a half miles and always in the Sunday cart. Reagan had been instructed to always keep them looking rough and unkempt and to let them do the whole lap of the field on the front leg, changing to the other leg lead, when they changed around to do it all again at which point. Reagan would add another half a sack of corn until both Daisy and Dandy were foaming and sweaty after each training session. Reagan would carefully record the time taken, in sheer wonderment as over the months each animal became faster and fitter.

The plan was going well and Reagan was calling in at Margaret's and taking Daisy and Dandy out twice a week, which made Margaret smile. She often cadged a lift into town to shop, or to be left in the *Royal Oak* for a catch up with her neighbours and friends, and again on Sunday to mass, always feeling the intense gaze of Monsignor Doyle's eyes wherever she sat in the church. Daisy and Dandy were looking good. Both had started to muscle up, and even Margaret had noticed how Dandy was filling out, and looking very much more the animal he should be.

Reagan on the other hand was not only still working his own blacksmith business, he was listening to every word his dear friend was telling him, eager to learn all the secrets. Miles, Tom's father, who in his time was a legend around the area, often treating horses and other animals with far more positive results than the local vets.

Tom's instructions were clear:

Feed – harvest the kale, turnips, carrots, chop and add to their hard feed. One tablespoon of molasses and linseed oil was to be added to their hot potato mash every Sunday. There was to be no fruit treats at all, the extra carrots, turnips and worzelmangels he had planted earlier that year, would bulk out the feed, and one day every week, he was to simulate the race and train them really hard. The day before he was to feed the kale and carrot tops in their food, a light mash only. On the day of the simulated race, there was to be no breakfast at all, and his father's special bitters was to be added to their water in the morning, and when they had finished that, their reward was a large bucket of mixed mash, with a spoonful of special mystery mix, which Tom had prepared before he left.

Training - much to Reagan's frustration, he had to use the Sunday cart only. He would drive them down to the one hundred acre field, the one used for the May Day celebration fayre, and occasionally other events. One by one, he would drive them around the field starting slowly at first, only to finish, turn around and go again, but the other way round, this way each side of the animals bodies were being muscled, and if Tom's suspicions were correct, this would help them race better and faster.

Reagan wasn't at all happy to long rein them, it was something he was uncomfortable with, and so with all the training going well, and 6 months into their planned schedule, he decided to call in on Ellie and Brendan, his dear friends; they would help him he was sure. Ellie and Brendan were absolutely delighted to see him, and especially Daisy. They rarely got to see how the stock they sold had worked out, and on seeing Daisy, both of them and their children who helped rear and train her were screaming with delight, kissing her nose, and stroking her with affection, which of course made Daisy do her little dance on the spot with all the excitement. The little dance sent them all into a delighted frenzy, as they remembered the very day Reagan had shod Daisy for the first time, and that little dance she did for them all.

"Oh, Reagan, how time flies!" said Ellie and Brendan. It was a sad, reflection filled moment, as they told Reagan of the death of Daisy's mother some months ago, and now seeing Daisy, they instantly fell in love with her again, and asked if she was for sale. They would offer a great price and have her back as breeding stock they told him, but it was to no avail, she wasn't his, or for sale, so with sadness they accepted they would never have her back. But things changed greatly when they put Dandy through his paces as they lunged him on the end of a long line. It was with sheer excitement at seeing this beautiful animal put through his paces that Reagan let slip the one secret he promised Tom he would never tell. With just Ellie and Brendan at his side, he told them of Daisy's night of passion with Legend, which actually sent them both into another hysterical moment, pleading with Reagan to go and ask Margaret if they could buy him. Five hundred guineas they offered, telling Reagan, Dandy was very special, had a brilliant pace, and turn of foot. However, once again Reagan had to refuse; he just was not for sale, and again he let slip that he was training them both to race at the festival race day, which was the day before the May Day fayre.

Ellie and Brendan, when they had finished lunging both animals, sat Reagan down with a slice of apple pie, and a cup of hot sweet tea, and got him to spill all the beans. Reagan in return swore them both to secrecy, and explained how dangerous it would be if it got out that Dandy was the offspring of Legend, and that even Tom and Margaret could be in danger if this information got out.

Of course they both agreed instantly, but not until Reagan had agreed to let Dandy mate two of their stock which were coming into season that week. They promised to pay a stud fee of course, if they both gave foal, and Reagan was happy that they would pay as they were honest, hardworking people who he loved very much. They also told him that they were struggling to find good new stock to bring into the herd, and on seeing Daisy and Dandy, they pushed him until he gave in.

Dandy mated both the female hinnies later that week and on the way home, Reagan suddenly realised that he had once again let his old friend down, and quite probably put all of their lives in danger. He hung his head with shame as he drove Daisy in through the cottage gate, with Dandy tied up at the rear. If Tom found out what he had just done and agreed to he knew after the last warning, he would probably kill him.

Chapter 9

Claire

TOM MANAGED TO GET HOME to Ireland every month now that the animals were in training. It was a fleeting and very tiring visit, arriving Friday morning, and leaving Sunday night, but Margaret was always delighted to see him. The farm was blooming, and crops were abundant; Margaret and the two animals would live well from her veg patch this year. He stood and marvelled at the two beautiful animals as they grazed in the darkening yellow orange sky, and suddenly a feeling of confidence enveloped him, and for the first time in ages, he felt at peace. His mind slowed, he took a deep breath in through his nose, and was calmed by the smell of his place, his land, Ireland, his beloved country. It was as though a spell had been waved over his head, calmness surrounded his being and he loved being there.

It all came to a sudden halt.

"Tom!" came the voice of Reagan from behind. Tom turned from where he was standing and looked over to the cottage from where Reagan was striding towards him. Tom quickly glanced back at the two beautiful animals. "Tom, how the devil are you?" Reagan asked outstretching his arm to shake his dear friend's hand. They shook in friendship.

"What a fine sight, friend, thank you so much," said Tom.

"Oh, Tom!" said Reagan shakily.

"What's up, friend?" Tom asked, his stomach now churning, realising a problem was about to emerge.

"Tom I've done something stupid, I have let us down, I am so sorry."

"For Christ's sake, Reagan, spit it out man!" said Tom.

"I've mated Dandy with two hinnies owned by my dear friends Brendan and Ellie. Tom they offered me five hundred guineas for him!" he blurted out, sweaty and really frightened of Tom's reaction.

"Reagan you stupid bastard, you've put us all in danger, what did I tell you?" he hollered back at him, shaking his head in disbelief that this so-called friend had totally done the opposite to what he had told him to do! He grabbed Reagan by the collar and pulled him close.

"Tom please, we can trust them, honest and if either of the hinnies produce a foal there will be a two hundred pound stud fee."

"Oh, Reagan what the hell did I discuss with you right at the very beginning of all of this?" he asked, feeling exasperated.

"Oh, Tom I know and I am sorry, I don't know what came over me," he responded forlornly.

"Right, Reagan, no more fuck ups or you'll have me to answer to, okay?" he asked him. "We'll probably have to dye Dandy after his race, the gypsies will want him!" he told him firmly; his eye contact told him everything.

***

CLEVER REAGAN, IN BETWEEN HIS blacksmithing work, had at last found a lovely lass, and married her. Claire O'Malley was in her late thirties and a widow, and had a lovely 6 year old son called Donal. Her husband, Nial O'Malley had been killed in an accident on a farm some 3 years ago, leaving her all alone with a 3 year old son in a small cottage on the outskirts of Gory. She was a handsome woman, with a mane of thick red hair, beautiful golden freckled skin, a great figure and deep blue eyes. She was some 5 years older than Reagan. Love blossomed one day when he was asked to attend to her sick and very lame goat.

Claire was very poor and took in washing and pressing for the more affluent families in the village, which in turn helped feed her and Donal as well as keep a roof over their heads. She would work all hours just trying to survive, often starving herself so her son could eat. The precious goat was her only source of milk, butter and cheese, and she was sick, really sick, so sick in fact that when Reagan called to see and attend to her, he really didn't know if she would survive. He also knew that she had no money for the vet, so he treated it the best he could and crossed every finger and toe, but he knew in his heart that it would probably die. She thanked him for his kindness with some home-made apple pie, just like his mother always made, which brought back painful memories of that dark, dark day after the Gory May Day fayre.

When Tom phoned later that week checking up on Daisy and Dandy and how the training was going, Reagan just happened to mention the sorry state of the goat, and his fears that the treatment he had administered would be nothing but futile. Tom knew instantly what the problem was, of course he did, he had dealt with his mother's goats all his life. He instructed Reagan to make up a special tea, with wild herbs and leaves which were in abundance in and around his own farm. This he immediately did, making double the amount so he could store some away in case it was needed again.

Claire was hanging the washing out when Reagan burst through the gate in his van, beeping his horn loudly to get her attention.

"Heaven, Reagan what's the distress?" she asked looking confused, worry creeping into her being at the sight of the very animated blacksmith who was jumping out of his van, and rushing towards her clutching a bottle full of green liquid.

“Claire how’s Matilda?” he enquired with excitement in his voice.

“Well, she’s still not up. What the devil have you there, Reagan?”

“Hopefully a cure. She’s got a nasty type of lungworm and we have to expel it, that’s why she’s not getting any better. My friend Tom Murphy has given me his secret elixir, shall we try it?” he asked her wide-eyed, admiring her curvy figure, and sexy, well-proportioned bosom.

“Oh, Reagan thank you, anything is worth a try,” she replied, dropping the washing into the basket and eagerly following him to the small shed where the poorly goat lay.

Reagan poured the whole bottle down the reluctant goat’s throat, whilst Claire held her steady, calmly reassuring Matilda that it was for the best, and that it was good medicine that would make her better.

“I’ll call around tomorrow and see how she is,” Reagan told her as he tipped his hat. Their eyes met in a silent, evocative, electric gaze.

“Please stay for a cup of tea, Reagan, it’s the least I can do as a thank you,” she said to him.

“Thank you, Claire, but I have clients waiting for me, and I am late already, but tell you what, I’ll be round first thing in the morning to check on Matilda, and I’ll have one then,” he replied, again tipping his hat, but not before reaching out and taking and kissing the back of her soft hand. His heart all a flutter he turned and jumped into his van, his knees weak and wobbly.

Claire on the other hand, for the first time since Nial had died, felt her heartstrings being pulled. When her beloved husband had died she had vowed never to look at another man, as he had been her first and only love. But there was something about this kind and gentle, caring man that stirred her womanhood, unsettling her, bringing back the longing she had to feel a man’s arms around her and waking in the morning next to someone. She also had a son, who needed a father, to love and guide him step into the world of manhood.

Many men had made advances towards Claire since she had become a widow, often placing their hands on her behind, and openly brushing against her buxom bosom, which repelled her, thinking of them as nothing but womanisers, just wanting her sexual favours, only then to move onto the next sad, lonely and frustrated widow.

Yes, Reagan Callow, you would make a good husband and provider for me and my son, breakfast it is then, she thought to herself slipping into a daydream, only to be brought out of it suddenly by the call of her demanding young son returning from his school day.

Reagan meanwhile, was all of a quiver. His head was in a whirl and for the first time in his life he felt a true attraction to this quiet, beautiful woman. It didn't matter to him that she was slightly older than him; he knew she was a good woman, hardworking, kind and true. He never listened to any of the gossip considering it to be nothing but jealousy, and thought she would make a good wife.

It was funny how the Lord worked his mysterious ways, sprinkling magic to make two people think the same thing, pulling them together.

"God, I must go home and have a bath tonight," he said to himself with excitement as he drove down the road to his next appointment.

Early the next morning, in fact very early, as promised, Reagan pulled in through the cottage gate.

"Oh my, Reagan, I didn't expect you so early, breakfast isn't ready yet!" she exclaimed all of a fluster as she had only just got up, and not even started to prepare the promised breakfast.

"Come on, let's go and see how Matilda is," he said pulling her by the hand, and saying a silent prayer in his head, as they made their way towards the small shed.

They both gasped with delight; Matilda was up and eating and greeted them with a loud bleat. "I am well!" it sounded like to both of them who started to giggle with sheer elation.

"Oh, my dear Reagan, how can I ever thank you?" Claire mumbled, as she stroked her dear friend's furry ears, tears now tumbling down her golden freckly face across her reddened cheeks.

"You can marry me?" he said looking at her. "Where the fecking hell did that just come from?" he suddenly asked himself. Now a worried look appeared on his gentle face and he was shaking inwardly to the core.

Claire gasped, and smiled back at him, her mind was also spinning. He had just done the very thing she had been praying for all night. A special smile just for him spread across her beautiful face. "Yes," was all she said, but in truth it was all she needed to say.

Reagan thought his heart would at that moment burst with joy and they both now had tears in their eyes. "I'll be a good husband to you and father to little Donal, you'll both want for nothing," he told her holding her hand and gently kissing the back of it.

"And I will be a good wife, keep a good home, and look after the both of you," she replied, now shaking with emotion, and quietly thanking the Lord above at the same time for answering her prayers.

Six weeks later they were married; it was a small affair just attended by twenty guests, at St. Mary of Magdalene, a small church just on the outskirts of Gory near Claire's home, then after to the *Royal Oak* for a sumptuous wedding breakfast. Claire and Donal soon settled into Reagan's lovely large farmhouse, bringing the lonely and unloved house back to life and making it a loving family home, just like it was when his parents were alive. He knew they would be so proud of him. Life for him now had a meaning, the one thing he had lost when his parents were suddenly taken from him that sad Sunday afternoon many years ago. But now he had a real family to support, a son to love and nurture, and a wife that needed his manly attention, and all of a sudden Reagan had become a husband, and a respected pillar of the community, and for the first time since his parents' death, he was very happy and content.

The serious job of getting Daisy and Dandy ready for the races carried on, and there was no honeymoon after the wedding. Claire had told Reagan they could always have a holiday sometime later, and she was actually more excited at the prospect of moving out of her little council owned cottage and into Reagan's large farmhouse, and starting again, making it their home, having a new wonderful life for her and her lovely son.

Reagan had excited her, telling her all about the little café his mother had started when she was alive; he totally convinced her that she could start it all up again, and resurrect the trade her mother had built. She was an amazing cook, and although he hated to admit it, she was even better than his mother. Claire's apple pie was truly amazing. Anyway, he didn't want her washing and pressing for the affluent families anymore, they had paid and treated her poorly, and she was his wife now, and very proud of that fact he was too, and he wanted to protect and give her the standing in life she deserved.

He also decided to adopt Donal, to make them a real family. He would teach him the ways of the forge, and he would become so good that he would be able to pass on his business when he retired, just like his father had planned to do with him. He reflected that his father would be so proud of him right now. He always felt like his father was with him, guiding him when he was planning for his future like for example, planning to ask Claire for her hand in marriage. He always felt his father's hand on his shoulder.

To Reagan it was a sign that he was doing the right thing, making the right decision, and when 3 months later Claire informed him she was with child – his child, his whole world changed and he knew that when he decided to ask Claire to marry him, the hand he felt on his shoulder had definitely been his father's. He had made the right decision to marry Claire, and now his life was complete, and so was his family. He was definitely the happiest man in the world.

Chapter 10

Back to Ireland

REAGAN'S NEW FANDANGLED, AS IT was to him, telephone, made contact with his friend Tom Murphy, in England so much easier. They could now speak weekly. Tom always called Reagan from Ma Brown's digs or from the red telephone box down by the pub at the bottom of the steps at home. Suddenly for Tom, the effort of having to write long, long letters of instructions for feeding and training eased. Quiet and secretive discussions made the plan start to fall into place and now for them all, a reality.

Reagan's mind was a whirl; the blacksmithing business was busy, but the great thing about it was, he could work around it, and as Tom had suggested, he said nothing to Claire about the intended races. She didn't need to know nothing, it was better that way, and what she didn't know couldn't hurt her, or so they thought.

Reagan had started making plans, big plans actually, alongside those Tom had instructed him on, writing absolutely everything down. He started by making the new lightweight aluminium shoes with little studs on the outside, along with the racing buggy, and the two lightweight bits for racing. Tom had very firmly and quite threateningly told Reagan, he must not use the racing buggy for training. That was so important. Reagan was becoming quite miffed that he couldn't use his new toys, but that was all in the plan. Why Reagan failed to understand that, made Tom worry constantly. Reagan wanted desperately to tear around the hundred acre field with Daisy and Dandy just to prove to Tom how fast they actually were, but if the gypsies spied what they were achieving there would be trouble, and very serious consequences, which was why both animals would stay pulling the Sunday cart. It was also why he wanted them to keep looking rough, which would actually not give anything away to anyone watching.

Tom had also told Reagan to be cautious at all times as he knew that one of the gypsy family members would be watching their every move, and report back to Patrick McConnell, who hated losing anything. He was a cruel, nasty, vile man and fifty pounds may as well be five hundred pounds as far as he was concerned, but the biggest thing was, that if they did win, the gypsies would want to buy and own Daisy and Dandy, and then race and breed them for themselves.

Tom was talking to Reagan on the phone one day when Reagan was being miffed about not using the racing buggy, Tom relayed his father's memories of many a time a gypsy horse was beaten by a really good farm horse or hinny and the owner refused to sell it to them, only to find it dead 2 or 3 days later with its throat cut, and all its hooves and ears cut off. It was the gypsy way of telling the winning owner, if we can't have this animal, then neither can you!

It was this little snippet of information that finally got through to Reagan's brain.

"Oh God, Tom," he replied, biting his lip with worry.

"So that's why we have to be so careful, Reagan, do you understand now?" he stated firmly.

The new racing buggy was painted green with bright red wheels just like the Sunday cart, which would also set well into the minds of Daisy and Dandy; it would cause no obvious excitement, they would just think it was a smaller Sunday cart, but in fact it was beautifully made, much lighter, and it handled brilliantly just as a racing buggy should. It had one small bench seat at the front, and the wheels were slightly stronger; it looked wonderful.

When Tom arrived back at Margaret's one weekend, they set off early in the morning to the hundred acre field, and after the tough but successful training session, called back into Reagan's yard, where Tom met his lovely Claire for the first time.

"Christ, Reagan well done, son, you have a lovely woman, remember to take care of her now mind you!" he told him.

"Oh God, Tom I will, I will," he nodded with a smile of affection on his face as Claire brought them out steaming hot tea and soda bread cheese sandwiches.

"Christ the buggy looks good, have you tried it out yet?" Tom asked. He threw the rest of what was left of the delicious sandwich into his mouth and muttered, "Lovely soda bread!" That from him was a real compliment.

Reagan replied irritated and quite animatedly, "You told me I couldn't!"

"You silly bastard, what's the matter with your brain, man?" he replied, raising his eyes up to the sky and clicking his tongue with despair. "You have a bloody fine and quick animal did you not have the bloody sense that you could try the bloody thing out with, Star?" Reagan sat and shook his head. "You, plonker, I thought you would have the sense to try him, he would love it, and he looks totally different to Daisy and Dandy, the McConnells would only think you were trying the cart out."

"Jesus, Tom that's brilliant, what a plod I am. I'll test it this very week, see how it runs and handles, make any adjustments that are needed," he replied with a smile on his face.

"Remember now, I'm off tomorrow, so when you are working them both with the Sunday cart, don't brush either of them, keep them dirty, it's hiding their new physiques."

***

THE WEEK OF THE RACE finally came around. Good weather was forecast for the weekend fayre which always took place on a Sunday. It was this time of year that always made Reagan feel so sad. Fond memories of his beloved mother and father would be uppermost in his mind. The crash and the day of their death never left him, and he often drove past the spot where it had happened that sunny and warm evening when they were on their way home after a lovely day out. Vivid images would always flash through his mind, especially those of his mother crying out in pain before she died, and his animal being shot at the side of the road. A little tear just for that second would creep out of the corner of his eye, he would then pinch himself, just to bring him back to reality, and thank the Lord above for the wonderful life he had now. He had his wonderful Claire and Donal, and of course the new baby to think and although he would never forget his parents or their place of death, his new family had helped mend the bare and painful wounds. The scars of sudden horrific death were a bastard to deal with, but now gradually with the help of a very large comfortable bandage in the form of his beautiful new family they were at last starting to heal.

***

TOM'S WIFE PATSY WAS INCARCERATED once again in Barrow Gurney Hospital. Her violent outbursts were at the moment, totally unmanageable, so her team of doctors felt it would be better for all, as she was beginning to make the family's lives unbearable, if she spent a little more time with them. They could then monitor her, check her lithium blood levels and try some new types of medication. This meant though that Tom had to take Megan and Trixie with him to Ireland.

They would be staying 5 days; it was all the time that Tom could spare, as he still had to work to pay the bills. However, he had been very savvy over the last few months, and had saved enough to pay the rent 3 weeks in advance, all the outstanding household bills, and still have enough for the train and ferry tickets. There was even enough left over to give his mother a nice little sum, and wager his fifty pounds bet. Once again he knew the demon would follow, so he would have to be on his guard.

It was the day they were leaving to return to Ireland, and Tom decided he would bless his home before he left and liberally sprinkled the inside of the house with holy water. This made the demon so angry that he screamed and shook the walls, his displeasure making the two girls laugh out loud, as they were used to his antics. This only served to make him even angrier and he knocked a picture of the Blessed Virgin Mary off the wall in the hall. It didn't matter though; this was his favourite picture to throw. The demon had broken the glass so many times during his demonic rages that Tom had cleverly had the glass replaced with some clear plastic, and had the frame re-enforced.

Tom smiled, said a little prayer, and then chuckled as he replaced the holy picture back onto the wall, before liberally sprinkling holy water over it, and all around the hallway. Then he and the two girls left for the train station.

IT WAS A LOVELY SMOOTH crossing, and the weary trio arrived at Rosslare harbour at five in the morning. Their little train to Gory sat in the station on a siding, right next to where the boat docked. They would be on time and arrive in Gory at precisely six that morning.

Johnny Byrne sat waiting in his now old and rusty, but very loved, red *Volkswagen* beetle. He jumped out of the car calling a greeting to them all, hugging and kissing the two girls with pride. It was a happy reunion; Johnny loved Tom and his family, and had the utmost respect for the way he often travelled home, and looked after his mother, so picking them up and depositing them back to the station on his trips, was nothing but a pleasure to him.

On the way to Margaret's house, they chatted excitedly, catching up on all the news, and putting the world right. Beep! Beep! Beep was the usual sound of the horn as they entered the little cottage gate, Daisy and Dandy instantly acknowledging their arrival, whickering loudly and trotting over to the gate in anticipation of the warm juicy apple they always received whenever Tom arrived.

Margaret appeared from inside the cottage. "Be Jesus, son, welcome, welcome. Oh, Megan and Trixie what a sight for sore old eyes," she cried, hugging and kissing them, watching Tom as he produced two warm apples from his pockets for the noisy and animated duo waiting at the field gate.

Johnny was invited in to share the feast that awaited the weary travellers on the kitchen table. Cold sliced chicken and ham, soda bread, butter and chutney, apple pie and cream, and lashings of hot sweet tea which was devoured with relish.

Now, on the journey over, Tom had sworn Megan and Trixie to a secret; all he had said was that he was taking Daisy and Dandy out for a few hours early Saturday morning. "Now, Granny will want to go to town, so I've arranged for Reagan to bring Star to the cottage so she could drive you all into town to go shopping." He went on to ask them both to really dote on their Nan and really look after her. He also reassured them there was nothing to worry about and that there was nothing underhand going on, so he wanted his mother to think nothing of the fact that he had taken Daisy and Dandy out for the morning. If they could do this little thing for him, it would be a worry taken off his mind.

They both agreed, loving the fact that they were back in Ireland with their Granny, back on the farm with the lovely veg plot and all the animals. Of course they would go shopping and dote on their gran, why wouldn't they?

Tom sighed and thanked them both; now all he had to do was make Saturday happen, then drive everyone with Daisy to the May Day fayre on Sunday. He suddenly felt a pang of guilt, remembering Tinker, Shamus and Patsy were all still at home in England. Subtle thoughts of the day he took Patsy and little Tinker to the May Day fayre when Patsy was pregnant with Megan, came flooding into his mind as did the gypsy woman's predictions. He shuddered, bringing him back to the now. It would be the girls first time at the fayre, and a grand day it would be. But there was another problem. The demon was on its way, he could feel it travelling towards them and it would be there that night, somehow he just knew it.

Chapter 11

The night before the races

TOM HAD A SLIGHT TOUCH of nerves the evening before the races. He was sat in his mother's cottage, with the two girls, the big race was tomorrow, and he had just sensed the arrival of the demon.

It was a lovely warm May evening, all was quiet, the cottage door was wide open, a lovely fire glowing in the hearth, and the leaves on the large oak tree outside were rustling in the breeze. But he felt foreboding.

He had spent the whole day planting corn and wheat which would start to come in the early spring; he had harvested the kale and spinach, and dug the last of the worzelmangels. He had been tending the beautiful veg patch which was starting to come alive with fabulous produce which would feed his mother and the animals all through the summer into the long cold winter months. The specially prepared racing tack for the new cart had been cleaned with saddle soap, until it was gleaming. Tom loved that smell; it always took him back to the days when he was a young boy, when he would attend the racing stables with his father. He would always stare in wonderment at the rows and rows of saddles and tack, all neatly in their place for each and every horse. The air was always filled with the smell of saddle soap, every item sparkled with cleanliness, and everything was always placed exactly where it should be.

Daisy and Dandy were both washed and groomed to perfection and this was one job that Megan and Trixie always loved to help with, both marvelling as they worked, at the change in the two beautiful animals they were attending, who loved all this special attention they were receiving. It was pure love all round, and a special moment for all.

Dandy especially stood out. You could see that Daisy was especially proud of her well-muscled son. Their manes and tails were pulled, and Megan and Trixie ran into the field to pick the white daisies to dress them with, just like they did for the wedding.

"No, no!" shouted Tom seeing them start to plait Daisy's mane. "You can't plait them up, it's not that sort of occasion," he gingerly explained hoping for no other questions about the next morning.

"That's okay, Dad, we'll give them to Gran, she can put them into a jam jar on the window sill," they both said leaving to present the bunch of wild flowers to Margaret, who was busy in the kitchen preparing the evening meal.

When he'd finished with the two animals, they both looked amazing. He then set about mixing their special race mix which he would give them tonight. They would wonder why there would be no breakfast in the morning though, so he decided before putting them both in the stable that night to talk to them and let them know that tomorrow was a special day, and that they would be staying in the stable tonight to keep them safe and secure.

He lit a large fire in the fire pit, and did the usual protection ritual, sprinkling holy water everywhere. He heard a growl in response and after seeing a pair of red eyes up in the oak tree, he ran back to the stable and blessed and sprinkled holy water all over it, chanting the exor chant, which in turn made the demon extremely angry, and very agitated. Once again, he found himself stuck in the tree.

Margaret heard the commotion and came running out into the yard. "Tom what ails, son?" she asked.

"Nothing, Mam, just sorting him out," he said pointing up to the oak tree which grew behind the cottage.

"Ah, he's here then, we all safe?" she asked feeling slightly nervous just for the moment.

"Oh yes, that's what all the noise is about," he replied, chuckling at the thought of that evil beggar stuck up in the tree unable to touch them. He hung brightly burning oil lamps either side of the front door as the light faded from the sky, built up the fire pit which would burn until morning, said goodnight to the world and locked the cottage door.

The slow roasted leg of kid was moist and succulent. Satiated and very full they all fell into bed that night tired and ready for sleep. Tom and Margaret recited extra prayers of protection for the safety of everyone, including his beloved Patsy and the two boys back in England, and Tom, especially for the next day at the races.

Chapter 12

Race day

EARLY NEXT MORNING WHILE TOM was busy standing outside brushing the speedy duo, having already cleaned the stable and tying them both to the field gate, Reagan pulled into the yard. Star, Daisy's brother was pulling Reagan's bright blue and yellow slightly smaller Sunday cart and Daisy whickered in acknowledgement of Star arriving.

"Quiet, girl," Tom whispered in her ear, waving at Reagan as he arrived.

"Are we ready, Tom?" he asked in eager anticipation.

"We are. Where's the sulky?" asked Tom.

"We'll pick it up when we pass the farm, I've to pick up their new bits and shoes as well," he told him, slightly nervous now, beads of sweat forming on his brow.

"Tie Star up outside the barn, there's a fresh hay net and water for him," Tom told him. "Mam knows what to do; he's only going to town today."

"Okay!" Reagan replied, tying Star up, giving him a lovely pat on the head, rubbing his ears and telling him to look after Margaret and the girls, which of course, he would.

The sight of the pristine green and red Sunday cart coming out of the stable got Daisy excited, and she danced her little dance on the spot with excitement. Her ears were forward and she was champing on the bit.

"Steady, girl!" Tom whispered to her.

She would pull the Sunday cart to the hundred acre field. Dandy was tied to the back and would follow them. Hay nets, water buckets, and all necessary tack needed for that day was stowed carefully under the back bench, and when both were satisfied they had forgotten nothing, they quickly and quietly left the farm. It was seven in the morning, and the sleeping trio they had left behind should be up in a couple of hours. Tom knew that Megan and Trixie would dote on Star, he was a good lad, and Margaret would drive him into Gory with ease. The two girls would keep their promise and keep her occupied as he asked them, making him feel a little easier. Looking all around before leaving, and without Reagan noticing, he sprinkled holy water everywhere, even over Star and his cart.

"Right, let's go now," he told himself, happy that all who were left behind were safe.

When they reached Reagan's farm, the sulky was parked to the side of the entrance gate.

"Reagan you've done a great job," Tom complimented him. A little brown pony about 12 hands high was harnessed to it. "She's nice, yours?" Tom asked him.

"Yes, thought we'd use her to mix things up a bit," he smiled, as he replied.

"Good thinking," nodded Tom, now starting to feel easier about what was unfolding. He loaded the cart with aluminium shoes for the races, and two small snaffle bits he had made, used mainly by racehorses so they were light in the mouth; he'd been trying them out on Dandy and Daisy with success. The big and bulky iron Pelham bits they used in general day to day work were heavy and rough, whereas these were strong and light, and both received and worked with them well. Tom was impressed. "Well, Reagan, if they're not ready now they'll never be," he told him.

It would be a nice steady one hour drive to the hundred acre field. Jenny, the small brown pony attached to the sulky, went ahead, driven carefully by Reagan, Daisy following behind pulling the Sunday cart. Suddenly Daisy shot into overdrive, trying to overtake little Jenny who was leading the convoy.

"Whoa steady, girl," Tom whispered to her, "you'll be having fun later."

She immediately responded, coming back to a gentle trot.

The races were due to start at midday, so they had 3 hours, which would give them time to get there, settle and rest, and most importantly, cast an eye on the opposition before the off.

***

MARGARET SPIED REAGAN'S CART OUTSIDE. Star's head was deep into a huge juicy hay net.

"Megan, Trixie, breakfast! Come on sleepy heads, chores to be done before we leave to get to Gory."

"Coming, Gran," came the reply.

It was a warm balmy May morning, and sunlight flooded in through the open cottage door. The fire was crackling in the hearth, and the crow of the cockerel rebounded all around the little yard as he called and scratched telling the other hens it was morning. It was the smell of the bacon frying wafting around the kitchen which brought the two girls running to the kitchen table, their hungry bellies asking to be filled, a high-pitched scream leaving their mouths and filling the air as they rushed past their breakfast which sat on the table.

"Star!" was all Margaret could hear as the two girls kissed and stroked his furry head.

"For God's bloody sake, you two! Breakfast!" called a now very irked Margaret.

“Oh, Gran he’s lovely,” they both said in unison, as they came back in and sat at the table now realising just how hungry they were.

Margaret was now fretting, worried something wasn’t exactly sitting right, and more annoyed that Tom had left this morning with no breakfast, not even a cup of tea.

“What is he up to?” she was asking herself quietly.

“Don’t worry, Gran he’ll be fine,” both girls blurted out together, now giggling, realising they had both heard Granny worry inwardly.

Margaret smiled to herself. “Chores, you two! Megan goats to milk, Trixie pigs and chickens to feed.”

“Okay,” came the reply.

Both girls were smiling as the eggs, bacon and mushrooms disappeared off the plate, washed down by strong, hot, sweet tea.

***

THE CONVOY ARRIVED QUIETLY AND totally unnoticed, just as Tom had planned. The sight was awesome, there must have been at least one thousand people milling around the amateur gypsy race track which was laid out in the field. The smell of the usual hog roasts filled the air, and there were at least five or six cider tents that Tom could see, already bursting at the seams. These would be used again tomorrow for the fayre day. The unusual addition of the race day meant a massive boost in business for the local innkeepers. A gathering of this amount of people for a special event such as this weekend meant thirsty people. The forecast for the weekend weather was hot and dry, and the cider tents were well stocked and the innkeepers were already toasting their good fortune.

They found a nice quiet spot under a large horse chestnut tree. Reagan jumped down from the sulky and reached into his tool bag, which was stashed under the seat. He retrieved a hammer and three large u shaped metal prongs, which he immediately struck into the trunk of the tree. He left enough space between them so all three animals could be tied up together under the shade of the tree's magnificent organic umbrella.

"My God, Tom." Reagan caught Tom's attention and pointed to the track; it was just as Tom remembered his father Miles telling him it would be, one and a half miles in a figure of eight. "Be Jesus, Tom, I understand now." Reagan now realised how silly he had been to even question Tom's knowledge.

"Yes, it's going to catch a lot of people out today, you need an animal that is used to trotting on either front leg, it's an old gypsy trick, they know how to make the opposition fail." He looked at Reagan and smiled. "Dear friend, let's hope all your hard work pays off today," he said as he rubbed Daisy down and then attended to Dandy, singing quietly to them as he worked.

Reagan meanwhile set about taking off their shoes and replacing them with the special studded aluminium shoes Tom had instructed him to make, which would really help both animals by making them more sure-footed, and safer.

Tom watched him work and said, "My God, Reagan how bloody good are you now?" Reagan's faced showed his pleasure at the end result; the shoes fitted perfectly.

Tom had to once again calm Daisy. "New shoes!" she excitedly announced dancing and whickering on the spot.

"Now, now, Daisy come on!" He stroked her muzzle lovingly, calming her instantly.

Meanwhile Reagan had wandered off into the crowds leaving Tom guarding the now quiet and relaxed duo. Jenny was in her own little world, she was used to being out and about with Reagan, and was totally unfazed with everything that was going on around her, and the large, sweet, hay net was definitely more interesting. She was actually very laid back, which was why Reagan loved her so much and was one of the best ponies Ellie and Brendan had ever bred. At forty pounds she commanded a hefty price, but Reagan considered her worth every penny. He never regretted buying her and she was able to take him out to farms and places that a van could not. She was very strong, reliable and sure-footed, and most of all, she was great friends and company for Star.

Once again, however, skulduggery was afoot, and Reagan had mated Dandy to her, and her belly was now swelling. Tom had noticed that Dandy was different this time around, and once mated young stallions can be hard to handle, but such was his beautiful passive and laid back nature, it hadn't affected him too much. Tom also noted Dandy trying to talk to Jenny and the swelling of her belly. He laid a hand on her and felt a little electric shock and knew she was with foal and that it was Dandy's.

Reagan, you and me will definitely be having words after this day is over, he promised himself.

Reagan soon returned with two large glasses of cider shandy, and the race timetable. Suddenly there was a commotion, Patrick McConnell, The General and his entourage had come to gloat, a trick they used trying to psyche out the opposition, but his face showed some concern as he eyed up the quietly content animals.

"Good day, Tom, ready to race?" he asked in a mocking tone.

The General was truly beautiful, a large stocky brown and white piebald stallion, standing some 15 hands plus, dwarfing both of Tom's animals. His mane and tail were thick and bushy, and he was beautifully turned out.

He's one fabulous horse, thought Tom.

The General's large wall eye stared at him, and the long driving whip hovered over his head, and it was then that Tom suddenly saw the fear in this animal. It always pained him to know that some of

God's most beautiful creatures were so afraid of their masters and their whip.

"How are you, Patrick?" Tom asked, totally unfazed.

Reagan stood from afar, watching and listening to the ongoing conversation, feeling very sick and wanting to wretch. The warnings that Tom had given him suddenly hit home and he now felt threatened. This man was evil, he could sense it, and visions of a cruel greedy man suddenly came into his mind. He turned and gently stroked Jenny, who acknowledged him with a loving nudge.

"Race three one o'clock – see you on the line!" Patrick tipped his hat and slapped The General hard, making him flatten his ears and bare his teeth. "Walk on, bastard!" he screamed at him.

Tom watched as the whole sorry entourage passed through.

"Fucking piece of shite," Reagan commented as they left.

"Umm, yes, don't worry he'll get his comeuppance," said Tom, quietly sitting at the bottom of the chestnut tree, sipping his shandy, thinking to himself, and contemplating his next move.

***

WITH ALL THE CHORES DONE, Margaret untied Star and with the help of the two girls, turned the cart to face the gate. Excitement filled the air.

Meanwhile the demon sat deep in the branches of the oak tree unable to move. The sunlight made him a prisoner during the day, and the holy water that Tom had sprinkled all around the little farm, literally over everything, prevented him from harming any of them at night. He was well and truly stuck, and very frustrated and angry. He would have to feed elsewhere tonight. He was hungry and feeling weak, but he would need all his strength to ambush and kill Tom Murphy. He would leave later, replenish his strength and return to finish the job that his first female, Patsy, could not.

Chapter 13

Under orders

THE RACING HAD BEGUN. TOM left Reagan in charge of all the animals, whilst he went to view the first race, warning him not to let anyone – absolutely anyone, near either of the racing duo. Gypsies would do anything to nobble a race if they felt threatened and would think nothing of slipping any animal a piece of apple laced with poison, or anything which would affect them and hinder their race. Oh yes, they could be bastards, and under no circumstances whatsoever was he to leave or take his eyes off of them.

Tom had seen quite a few unknown people passing by, studying their steeds, and worry was setting in, but he had to go and view the track, see how it drove, and spot any problems or areas of concern that could arise.

Unremarkably, the first race was won by the gypsies, the black and white trotter driven by Jimmy Mackintyre having walked it. The horse was well muscled and used to racing on either front leg, around left or right handed tracks. The beautiful chestnut driven by Eileen McCotter stood no chance. It was a right handed track racer, and only racing twice a year at the Furnleaze race park in Donegal, she was used to winning, but as suspected, her chestnut couldn't cope with the figure of eight track and trailed in at least half a furlong behind, much to the disappointment of Eileen. She had really fancied her chances, laying a hefty one hundred pound bet on herself to win.

THE NEXT RACE WAS INTERESTING, WITH TWO large hinnies just like Daisy, well trained and muscled. It looked like a fair race between two well matched animals, but again the gypsy hinny, although slightly smaller, won well, and Tom noticed from the front, the top left hand corner would win or lose you the race, and that again the hinny that won, was trained on both legs. He was next up so he quickly went back to Reagan. Daisy was already harnessed to the sulky and doing a little dance on the spot with excitement.

The crowd had thickened, bookies were busy, and business was brisk, huge amounts of money changing hands. A large black board at the start line announced *The General-v-Daisy*, the next race. Gypsy gold was flowing; they used it as a form of money. The glint of the soft coloured metal flashed around in the crowd and especially the finish line where the crowds thronged together, eager to see the outcome of the forthcoming battle. Everyone knew that Tom Murphy was putting his head on the line, and absolutely no one was betting on him. Heavy money piled into the now worried bookies on The General to win, some betting a walk over, or even a non-finish.

"Right, lass let's go," said Tom quietly.

Daisy acknowledged him, chomping on her new light bit, and if you could see her, you would have seen that she was smiling! She loved the feel of the new light bit in her mouth, and the safe feel of the lightweight studded shoes. "I'm ready, I'm ready, Master Tom," she was chuntering to herself, trying to keep all her excitement under control.

"Right, Tom are ye okay?" asked Reagan nervously, as they were leaving for the start, beads of sweat forming on his brow.

"We'll be fine won't we, girl? Have you paid the fifty pound wager to McConnell?" Tom asked him.

"Aye, they called for the payment. Have you betted, Tom?" Reagan asked him with interest.

"Aye," he replied.

"Well what did you bet?" Reagan asked him, now wide-eyed and anxious, trying to calm himself by rubbing Dandy's furry ears.

"Wait and see," he smiled as he replied, and gently pushed Daisy off in a brisk walk towards the start line, asking Daisy to be calm. He had a plan. "Just enjoy," he told her with his whisper magic. His own nerves though were wracking through his body as the crowds in front of them parted, all the men lifting their hats to him in respect and admiration of his quest, but there could be no other outcome they all agreed. The General would win.

The crowd was enormous, twice as big as anticipated by the organisers, who were themselves rubbing their hands together with glee. The entrance fee alone that the punters paid was enough to pay for the rent of the field for the next 3 years and keep this race day going. God if only they could have someone like Tom Murphy, willing to put his head on the line every year! They were convinced this had pulled in the crowds that were now all crammed at the start and finish line.

A nervous anticipation filled the air. McConnell had challenged Tom to a race, and it was just about to start. The crowd was watching, and nervously expecting a complete walkover by The General, everyone eagerly waiting to receive their bundles of winnings from the sweating and anxious bookies. Quite a few had now closed their books, fearing they didn't have enough cash to pay out on the win and angry betters fuelled with rough cider, were now shouting and becoming very irate at not being able to place a bet.

The two animals finally arrived at the starting line; every race was properly conducted and judged by course stewards from the local race courses, and they were all completely neutral. Unpaid or nobbled by the gypsies, no one knew who would be arriving or assigned to each meeting, keeping their identity safe, and unreachable.

Rory Callaghan was one of the most senior stewards assisting that day. “She looks good, Tom, can she do it?” he asked, smiling as The General pulled alongside Daisy, dwarfing her. Of course, he’d seen it all before, he’d been a steward for 20 years, but there was something about this little hinny that made him smile, and take a breath. Something told him The General, just could have a race on his hands today.

“We’ll see,” Tom replied with a little smile. “Looking good!” he said acknowledging McConnell who was busy gathering up his long whip ready to strike The General who was fidgety and raring to go. “Be calm, girl,” Tom whispered to Daisy as she reacted to the snorting, prancing, bit chewing, eye rolling, giant at the side of her, which was exactly what McConnell wanted.

The General was now blowing hard and pawing the ground. McConnell’s eyes flashed at Tom and a nasty grin on his face told Tom he just could be in trouble.

Chapter 14

Ghost town

STAR PULLED THE LITTLE BLUE and yellow Sunday cart beautifully for Margaret. He looked quite similar to Daisy, but slightly smaller and he had a little white star on his forehead. Margaret smiled as she drove them into town, Megan and Trixie waving to the few people they encountered on the way. It seemed exceptionally quiet. It was Saturday and usually Gory was teeming with folks all rushing around, getting in their weekly supplies, then meeting up at the *Royal Oak* to catch up on all the gossip, and news from far and wide. Only those who were more affluent had radios. Margaret would have loved one, as it would have kept her and Daisy company. Instead of having to go into town every week and rely on other people's news, she would be able to hear it all first hand.

"Right, that's it, I'll have a word with Tom when he gets back," she chatted to herself quietly, as Star gently trotted on, and the beautiful countryside passed them gently by.

Gory was empty! They were the only people as far as the eye could see, it was like a ghost town, and even the *Royal Oak* was closed. They tied up outside *O'Reagan's*, her now usual large grocery store. Thanking Star for all his hard work, Megan and Trixie quickly alighted with a hay net and a bucket from behind the cart. The bucket was filled from a large old stone trough which was filled with clear rainwater, just a few yards down from where they were tied up. With Star settled and happily munching away the trio headed for the store, grabbing a shiny new trolley on wheels on the way in.

"Well what in heaven ever next?" Margaret said in disapproval of another fandangled new contraption.

"It's okay, Gran, we have these in *Fine Fare* back home, you put all the shopping into it, and take it to the till, it makes your shopping easier," Megan told her.

Trixie was giggling in the background, and she caught a stark stare from a very irked Margaret, which made her quieten straight away. Trixie bit the inside of her lip, looking away down the aisles of food, still trying not to laugh as they proceeded around the enormous market.

Roast beef was on Margaret's mind. They soon found the butchery department. It was the hundred acre fayre the next day, so she would leave ham hocks bubbling away, which would be ready to eat when they arrived home, but she fancied beef that night. God only knew the last time she had eaten beef, she could never afford it, but today her purse was full as Tom had given her an extra thirty pounds. She would stock up the larder and buy a nice piece of brisket. She eventually chose a nice long, fatty piece that she knew would slow roast really well, two ham hocks, fat bacon, sausages and four pork chops. She was satisfied with her meat selection.

They ambled around the quiet almost deserted store and had the time and the space to look at all the new and wonderful rows of food, some that even Megan hadn't seen before. It felt eerie and odd. Normally the store was full of bustling people, always uncomfortable, and you had to push through the squashed in crowds, but not today.

"Margaret!" came the call from shop assistant Noleen O'Brien.

"Oh hello, Noleen where is everyone today?" she asked her.

"Oh, we were rammed yesterday; the gypsies are racing today at the hundred acre field, so everyone shopped yesterday. You would have hated it, Margaret so enjoy the quiet. I see you have some of the best meat off the counter today, I'll make sure you get a ten percent discount on your butchery when you check out for being one of our best and loyal customers." She winked at her as she was passing, admiring the two young girls that accompanied her. "Is this Megan and Trixie?" she asked her quizzically.

"Why yes!" replied Margaret proudly, but her mind was now whirling, the penny had just dropped.

"My, what beautiful young ladies, grown so much, I hardly recognised you both. Your dancing at the wedding was amazing. Do you still attend Deidre Daniels' dance classes?" she asked, but Margaret did not give the girls the time to reply.

"Got to go, Noleen, thank you!" She turned and hurriedly pushed past with the two giggling girls pushing the trolley.

It all made sense now. Reagan, bloody Reagan, coming and taking Daisy and Dandy out for all these months, Tom not there that morning, Star tied up outside.

Margaret was furious and now started to fret. *What if Daisy comes to any harm?* she thought to herself.

"Don't worry, Gran," said Megan, almost as if she was reading her thoughts, "my dad loves Daisy and Dandy, he would never let anything happen to them."

Margaret turned and looked at her two beautiful granddaughters and smiled. "You're right, but I just wish he had told me, these gypsies can be bastards," she told them. "God only knows what would happen to my Daisy if she won any race, because that's what they are doing, I am sure they are bloody racing!" she said still fretting.

Margaret finished her shopping, it was all loaded in to the back of the cart, and the three of them once again set off for home. Margaret suddenly appreciated just how strong Daisy was, as Star seemed to struggle up the hill, but at the top, she let him have his head and trot at a nice pace along the long road to home. He began to eat up the miles and the stony lane soon came into view, before he eventually stopped outside the front door.

"Girls unharness Star and put him in the field, he's worked hard," Margaret instructed them as she unpacked her purchases, and headed into the cottage, feeling the glare of the demon in the oak tree.

Megan and Trixie screamed with delight as Star bolted around the lush green field, almost instantly finding the dust pit and rolling and rolling in sheer delight.

The brisket of beef was placed on a large trivet over a deep pan, rubbed with salt, pepper and mustard. Clean rainwater was placed under the joint over sliced onions and leeks; this would slightly steam it so it would be soft and succulent, and any juices in the bottom pan, along with the softened veg would be used for gravy.

While Margaret prepared the beef, Megan and Trixie peeled and thinly sliced the potatoes. Each slice was dipped in dripping, and layered with salt, pepper, finely sliced onions and chopped rosemary. The potatoes were packed tightly in a metal tin which sat at the side of the hearth; they would slowly cook and form a beautiful potato cake, soft and succulent. The vegetables would be pulled from the garden later, and Megan made up a batter which would sit, and cook for the last 20 minutes for the Yorkshire pudding. Gravy made with butter and flour was the last chore; this would balance the meal to perfection.

Margaret meanwhile was still trying not to panic. "Girls," she called.

"Coming, Gran!" was the reply.

"Chickens to feed, oh and give the pig some swill," she instructed. "And if you want pudding, you had better go and find something!" she called as the kettle started to boil. Her mind was still whirling, and she was praying and fingering the rosary hanging from her belt asking the Lord to bring her beloved Daisy and Dandy back home safely.

Chapter 15

Daisy's Showdown

DANDY AND I WERE EXCITED. We had loved all the attention the kind man Reagan had been giving us over these last months. We both loved running. Dandy is so much faster than me. He loves me, and he often tells me how proud he is that I'm his mother. We are both so fit and well. Perhaps today we will run, I quietly told Dandy as we were standing together under the large shady tree. I told him how I used to run around the field as a youngster, always winning. I loved to win, I told him.

We could sense the excitement in the air, and the roar of the crowd in the distance made me nervous, but not Dandy, he was well chilled out as always. Reagan approached.

"Come on, lass, it's your turn now," he quietly said as he tacked me up.

Both Dandy and I agreed that the new small bits are better, as is the small cart I was to pull.

"Oh gosh, it's so small, how much fun will this be?" I excitedly called to Dandy, who just looked over and smiled his horsey smile.

Master Tom arrived back, and after a few quiet words with Reagan, we were off, pushing through the crowds, Master Tom whispering in my mind telling me to stay calm. We finally reached a post and line. I could see a tall man wearing a hat, a flag in his hand, standing on top of a tall chair. The field lay out before us. The noise of the crowd rumbled all around in the background, as Master Tom spoke with the man in the hat.

I realised I was shaking, my legs were wobbling and I wanted to be sick. I wanted to run now! The long, figure of eight course looked inviting. I could see myself running up that hill. I knew where I was and recognised that this is where Dandy and I had trained with Reagan, and excitement gripped me.

"Steady, girl!" Master Tom again whispered to me.

A large brown and white horse pulled up beside us. He had a piercing blue and white wall eye and he stared deeply at me. He was menacing and massive.

"Prepare to lose," he shrieked.

"Lose? I never lose, I always win," I whickered back.

He pawed the ground with anger and anticipation, and threw his head around in defiance, his long shaggy mane magnificent and flowing.

"I always win," I again told myself. The large ugly man on the cart next to me raises his whip to the agitated monster wriggling beside me.

"Are we going, are we going?" I asked Master Tom excitedly.

"Soon, Daisy soon. Be calm. Remember, no cantering, flat out extended trot, just as Reagan trained you," he told me, but excitement had taken over and I wasn't listening. I had to win, just had to. This brute didn't frighten me, I knew I was faster, the angels had told me so.

The flag was raised in front of us. "Ready!" called the tall man with the hat on looking at us both sternly – then it dropped!

The General pulled forward like a train, he was already anticipating the painful lashes from his master he always received when racing. He was used to this cruelty, the scars on his back had hardened, and the lash of the whip didn't hurt so much now, except when he lashed his neck catching his eye; that was so painful, producing bleary tears, which made racing more difficult.

Unfortunately Daisy broke straight into a canter. This was against the rules, so Tom gently circled and calmed her, and once again let her go.

"Flat out extended trot," he was telling her, pushing her on, giving her confidence, and telling her she could catch him, and still do it.

Her mistake had let The General get away, he was a good 500 yards ahead, but she was flying, eating up the ground with every stride, and knew what to do. She could hear the crowd screaming, laughing out loud at the sight of her trailing in the wake of the brown and white monster, but Daisy was loving the race, and her pace again quickened. It was as though all she had was a feather on her back, not the heavy Sunday cart. She was flying and eating up the ground, and very quickly closing up the gap, and this was where all the training would finally click in.

As they passed the post on the first lap, she was now only about 150 yards behind, and the crowd was becoming anxious.

"This bloody thing is catching The General!" a terrified cry came out of the crowd, everyone now leaning forward, craning their necks forward to get sight of the power struggle on the course. The ticktack men were now signalling frantically to the bookies, which were all stood quietly, most with their heads in their hands, just thinking about all the cash they would soon be paying out.

McConnell was laughing out loud when he saw Tom circling Daisy, easily letting him get away. "It's a walkover!" he screamed out loud, raising his whip in the air, but shock ran through him like a sharp knife when he heard Daisy coming, and oh God was she coming fast.

Tom was amazed. "Brilliant, girl, you can do it!" he was calling now to her, feeling the power flow through the reins to his hands.

As if by magic, you could even call it heavenly magic, the little cart flew. McConnell started to panic, wildly thrashing The General. There was only half a mile to go and on the straight, and Daisy was almost with him. The crowd had now been whipped up into a frenzy and had never seen anything like it. The General was giving it his all, now blowing hard and pulling with all his might, but Daisy was still coming and she was quicker. She loved every minute, every stride, and every push.

By now they were neck and neck, with 500 yards to go. McConnell thrashed out and hit Daisy hard on the back.

"Bastard, fuck off!" Tom called. He had no whip, he didn't need one. McConnell now barged his cart into Tom's making Daisy veer to the side, losing valuable ground, and The General again pulled ahead. "Go on, girl get him!" Tom screamed out in rage for everyone to hear, and Daisy did just that. Seemingly from nowhere she found another gear, quickly making the ground back up.

The winning line was in sight. The General was blowing hard and covered in foam. McConnell had thrashed the life out of him, and bloody, foamy flecks splattered all around the racing duo, on the cart and on Tom and Daisy. They were now neck and neck again, and McConnell was thrashing and screaming at The General but he could give no more, and Daisy was still there. The crowd was going berserk, and screams filled the air.

"General! General!" boomed out from the worried crowd as the pair flashed past the winning post.

Reagan in the meantime had been watching from a vantage point at the top of the field, Dandy standing quietly beside him. "Go on, Daisy!" He was also screaming at the top of his voice, seeing the whole race unfold before him. "My God, what a gal!" he again screamed as loud as he could, but to no avail, it was bedlam down on the track below, no one would have heard him. He turned and took Dandy back to the tree for shade and safety.

Tom pulled Daisy gently to a stop and turned back towards the post. McConnell pulled The General to a violent, sudden and harsh stop. The

General collapsed and died instantly. The animal had given everything, even its life for his vile, cruel master. McConnell was thrown from the cart, but the horse tumbled over trapping him underneath. The sickening sound of McConnell's legs breaking echoed all around the track, and screams and moans emerged from the bewildered crowd, who were all wondering what the hell they had just witnessed. This terrible scene had unfolded from a brilliant race, and no one even knew what the result was, it was absolute mayhem.

"Draw!" came the result announcement. The course stewards had quickly huddled together discussing the race. They had seen McConnell try to drive Tom off the track, but they were fearful of the wrath the gypsies could bring. Massive money had been bet, most of it lost, and the fairest thing all round, and to avoid a riot was to declare it a draw, even though everyone agreed the hinny's nose was slightly in front, and that if she had not had to circle, she would have easily outrun The General, so a draw it was deemed.

McConnell was pulled out from under the dead animal that had given his life for the race, but not before one young man, obviously a stable lad, had ran over to where McConnell lay in agony, and kicked him as hard as he could in his already shattered legs, causing him to pass out immediately. The lad had big bumbling tears in his eyes and was distraught at the sight of the dead horse that he clearly loved.

It was a sad sight, seeing the knacker man loading the broken body of The General onto the back of his lorry. As always, he attended every race. Racing always brought danger, as in life there could possibly be death, it was a known factor, one horse would die at every meeting, and it was his job to clear away the animal, or dispatch it quickly, diligently, and with as much respect as possible. He had seen The General run and win many a time, and you know, even a knacker man has feelings. A little tear was always shed whenever a good horse went down, and today was one of those days!

The bookies were raising their hands up in the air, and praying out loud, thanking the Lord above for the most wonderful result. Who would have ever thought an unknown farm hinny could draw with The General, Ireland's famous winner?

Disappointment ran through the crowds of punters. Thousands and thousands of pounds had been lost on that race, not to mention the hoard of gypsy gold that sat gleaming in piles at the feet of the bookies, who were now ecstatic, all promising better odds on the next three races, especially the last race, the open. They were confident that as it stood there was no opponent for Ireland's reigning champion 'Legacy'.

"MY GOD, TOM THAT WAS brilliant, I thought you got it you know!" Reagan cried kissing Daisy on the nose. She was hardly puffing, she was so fit.

"Aye, bastard got his comeuppance, though it's a shame about The General, could have been a brilliant horse in kinder hands," he replied sadly, suddenly thinking about the crumpled brown and white body on the course. "Thank you, Reagan you have done wonders with these two. She would have won you know!" Tom proudly commented looking at him and smiling as he jumped down from the sulky, before gently pulling Daisy's ears. "Thank you, girl, well done you were amazing," he told her with sheer admiration of her efforts today.

"It was a great race, Tom, what about the open?" Reagan asked getting a large bucket of water and a juicy hay net for Daisy, which was well received. She buried her head immediately into the bursting ball of sweet hay.

"What's the opposition?" Tom asked.

"Legacy," Reagan nervously replied, trembling at the thought.

The crowd had gone back to fever pitch, another race was underway, and their roar could be heard in the background. Tom meanwhile was deep in thought when a member of the McConnell family, a small red haired young man, appeared riding a pretty small palomino pony.

"Tom Murphy!" called the young man sat astride the sweet natured animal, who was very interested in Daisy, putting out her nose to acknowledge her, which Daisy accepted.

"Who's asking?" Tom replied.

"Kevin McConnell, Patrick's son. Would you please accept our apologies for the way Da conducted himself in the race no harm meant? Here's your money, one hundred pounds, if you want to sell the hinny we'd be interested."

I bet you would, thought Tom.

"Five hundred guineas," the young man offered.

"She's not for sale, son, but thank you anyway," he replied. The young man tipped his hat and turned to go, it was obvious he had been crying and pain covered his babyish face. "Kevin," he called out as he turned to face him, "he was a great horse, he gave his all, be proud, son," he told him.

"Yes, sir," he replied, wiping a tear from his soft brown eyes on his sleeve, and leaving as quickly as he had arrived.

"Tom Murphy!"

"Oh what the bloody hell now?" spat Reagan, as a dapper looking gentleman in a trilby and a fine tweed suit appeared from the thicket. It was Miles O'Leary the bookmaker Tom had placed his bet with. He smiled a broad Irish smile as he passed across his winnings, two hundred pounds.

"How in God's name did you know it would be a draw?" he asked in sheer amazement.

"I knew Daisy was super fit, and she's never raced before, it's a novice thing, and I expected McConnell to try and cheat when he realised just how quick Daisy was. I knew he'd panic. Shame about The General though," he replied with a heavy heart.

"Are you racing the open? I'll give you good odds, the best, what you got?" O'Leary asked in earnest.

Tom looked over and pointed to Dandy. The bookie gazed at the young stallion with its large floppy ears and tongue hanging out to one side of its mouth and said, "You racing that?" He was shaken and didn't believe his eyes. "I'll offer fifty to one to win."

"I'll take it," said Tom handing him over one hundred pounds.

"And me!" chirped up Reagan, passing over one hundred and fifty pounds. "Tom, I'll go and register Dandy!" he excitedly shouted, leaving immediately and running all the way to the stewards' tent to declare his entry, already feeling the pound notes in his pockets. "Oh my God, Lord above, please let Dandy win," he prayed out loud as he ran as quickly as he could.

Miles turned and looked at Daisy. "Tom that's some beast, careful now you know the gypo's will want her," he warned him.

"They've already offered five hundred guineas for her, and I told them at the outset, she is not for sale."

"And what about that?" he said pointing to Dandy.

"Good little lad out of Daisy," he replied.

"Well good luck, Tom, Legacy is all of Ireland champion and a fabulous animal, and fast. It's never been beaten."

"Well we'll have a little go, just like Daisy, first time out, I think we can give him a run for his money," he said smiling and feeling quietly confident.

"Well good luck, I hope I pay you out, we've had a brilliant day, and I never mind paying an honest and worthy winner," he smiled, tipping his hat and returning back to his stand at the start.

Chapter 16

Dandy's race

REAGAN RETURNED PUFFING, HIS RUDDY cheeks beaming, showing he had run all the way back from the stewards' tent with sheer excitement.

"All done, last race, three o'clock."

"Right, not long then, let's get Dandy ready," he told him, while untacking Daisy, and again thanking her for all her hard work. He tied her to the tree where she could finish the hay net and tuck into a small bucket of treats he had prepared for her earlier.

Dandy just quietly took everything in his stride, not really worrying about being hitched up to the new small cart, really, it meant nothing new. His light new shoes felt tight, and good, and he wondered where he would be going now. Daisy meanwhile gave a little whicker, telling him he would be racing at the one hundred acre field, the very field that Reagan had been taking them to and training them in.

"You'll love it," she told him.

Suddenly his ears pricked up, his stance changed, and his tongue retracted. At that moment, Tom saw something in this animal change, and just for one split second he saw the Legend, his father in him, and an electric shock flew down his spine.

Fuck, we could win. The thought suddenly entered his mind. He could also read Dandy's mind, just like Daisy's, and he could tell that he wanted to win, but Legacy, could he really do it, he wondered.

"I can win," Dandy replied looking over at an astounded Tom, his eyes doing all the talking, acknowledging what lay ahead.

Tom suddenly realised that this animal actually had no fear of losing, something that had been passed down from his sire. An angel suddenly passed by with a large sword in his hands.

"Oh, Jesus!" he muttered. He had been so engrossed with the races that he had totally forgotten about his mother and the two girls back at the cottage. "You keep them safe please until I get home," he asked them in his mind, bowing at the angels who were listening to his request and bowing back in acknowledgement.

"Reagan!" Tom called. "Let's get this thing done and get out of here as quick as possible."

"Righto!" came the response, a massive smile appearing on his face as he watched Tom alight into the sulky and once again push through the humming crowd to the start line.

Dandy had suddenly come alive and he pranced beautifully, stretching out into long perfectly balanced strides, almost like a dressage horse, totally showing off his beautifully crafted and hard worked muscle. This was a stallion thing, and he knew exactly what to do. The punters went quiet, shocked by what they were seeing. Surely this wasn't the same animal that Miles O'Leary the bookie had been laughing about earlier? His ears were pricked high, and his face was serious – it was a winner's face.

Toms psyche rocked and shook, just as if a bolt of lightning had gone right through his core. The crowd went quiet, and the bookies started to slash the odds as this amazing looking duo passed by. He was a mean looking piece of horseflesh, and you know what, Dandy knew it. He also knew he was going to race.

Reagan watched again from his viewing point, Daisy at his side, almost wetting himself with anticipation and pride. He knew this animal was good, really good, just like his father, and this, he suddenly realised, would be a race to remember, possibly the only race this animal would ever have, but by God would it be a good one!

Suddenly feeling sick with excitement and suspense, he thought about the two hinnies he had mated on Ellie's and Brendan's farm, and Reagan's lovely Jenny. Oh, God! He suddenly felt faint. He was in the money and he felt it. A dash of fear hit him like a bolt to the head - he would have to own up about Jenny, it wouldn't be fair, Tom was the most honest and honourable man he had ever had the privilege to know. He decided immediately, there and then that whatever the outcome he would confess.

It had been a massive success for the gypsies, only Daisy's race which was declared a draw, tainted their race card, most of them winning back their gold, which actually the bookies didn't mind. Gypsy gold was worth more to them than to the bookies, for whom cash was always king, but to the gypsy families, their gold showed their wealth and worth.

The death of The General had been a great shock and loss but as the other races were won and lost, he soon faded into memory, as did McConnell's injury. It served him right, many said. There would be other Generals in the future, better even than he. They were all looking forward to the final race, in which a fabulous stallion that no one had ever beaten was to race. Usually no one ever challenged him and most of his races were a walkover, where he would parade and just walk the course in front of everyone, who would admire this amazing horse.

Today, however, a man called Tom Murphy had put down the baton, the challenge, and there was no prize money at stake, just the title, fastest trotter in Ireland, and Legacy had held that title for the last 4 years.

THE MASSIVE BLACK STALLION STOOD quietly and passively on the start line. Thomas O'Donnell sat in his cart, pride bursting out of his skin at the sight of his black monster in front of him. Like Tom, he carried no whip. Tom studied him as they approached sensing a fair race.

"Tom O'Donnell," he said to Tom reaching out his hand to acknowledge them as they arrived.

"Tom Murphy," he replied, shaking his hand. He liked the feel of this man's handshake.

"Here's to a good race, Tom," he said, immediately feeling unruffled. He also knew that Tom Murphy was a whisperer, but on looking at Dandy, something stirred inside him. Instantly his being was invaded with uncertainty. Not for one moment did he doubt the speed of his horse, but today, it would be a race, a proper race. Normally it would be a no-show, or even a complete farce, as nothing had ever matched Legacy, for speed, stamina, or even his beauty, but today something told him for the first time in years it would!

"Good luck, gentlemen," said the tall ginger haired course official, raising his hat to them both in sheer respect.

Both animals were now pawing the ground, their eyes afire, bright and focused on the job in hand. Dandy suddenly looked every part of what was his being – a racer.

Tom gulped and suddenly asked the angels and the Lord above for guidance, and all he heard was a word that would probably stay with him for the rest of his life – trust! So at that one point in his life, and for the very first time, Tom decided to do that very thing.

The flag went down and both animals pulled away from the start line. The sheer power of these beasts was unbelievable, each having a look of love in their eyes. You have to love to race to do it, and they did, their hooves pulling massive force through the clay soil underneath, sending up large clods in their wake. The momentum took the drivers almost through into a special kind of space that only they would know, which was why they raced, it was a unique feeling not known to many, and both drivers were taken away up into their own stratosphere.

They both suddenly came back from their special internal dream state. Tom O'Donnell was whistling and calling to Legacy to push on, as he knew that the first to the top left hand corner would control the race, and usually the race was lost or won right there, but Tom was calm, and Dandy knew exactly what he was doing. The two animals came around the bend, Legacy ahead, but only just. You could hear a pin drop; the only audible sound was the thud of the horses' hooves tearing through the earth, their snorting and breathing as they worked and the whistles and shouts of Tom O'Donnell. The crowd was silent, holding its breath, betting slips being crushed in sweaty palms, prayers rising up into the clouds in their thousands, as everyone strained to watch this king of all races. It was a magnificent sight, two powerful animals running in unison; it was almost a vision of beauty. The line came into view and they flashed past the post, first circuit done, Legacy still in front, blowing and sweating, and still pulling like a train.

Unexpectedly, tears formed in Tom's eyes, as a surge went through his body. "Steady, son!" he called to Dandy, calming his stride. He knew that Dandy was playing with Legacy, and he knew he could take him. "Oh, dear God," Tom mumbled, tears falling in rivulets, as he released the reins.

Dandy didn't need telling what to do, he already knew. Both horses made it to the top bend again, then the right hand turn, half a mile to the finish; there was nothing in it. Murmuring whispers flowed around the subdued crowd, and a sudden scream was let out by one worried punter. "Dandy's going to take him!"

"Oh, no!" the crowd reacted in sheer shock and horror, the cries rebounding all around the field especially at the winning line where most of them had gathered. They could see the two carts at the top of the hill, they were side by side, still absolutely neck and neck, and it was as if the whole race was happening in slow motion.

Tom felt like he was in a dream, but the dream felt real. He could see his father Miles, at the winning post, smiling, waiting for him to bring Dandy home.

"Careful, son, bring him home safely," he heard him say in his head, wise words from a wise man.

Tom felt like he was flying, Dandy's large strides pulling the cart as though it was travelling through the air. They were alone now, just he and Dandy, and he wasn't aware of anything else. He was alone with Dandy in a remarkable silent world of speed and effortless motion, just as if he was in an emotional cloud.

The roar of the crowd brought the dream to an abrupt end. As Tom had suspected, Dandy had just been toying with Legacy, and had run his own race, passing the now tiring black stallion on the top bend, and extending his stride so much that he left him standing. It was a glorious sight to see, Legacy had been truly thrashed.

The shock on Tom O'Donnell's face was there for all to see. He was beaten, Legacy just could not match the turn of speed Dandy had produced, and a quiet tear crept from the corner of the old man's eyes. He of course always knew that this day would come, but he had hoped it would not be so soon. Still, Legacy had enjoyed four undefeated years, more than any other horse ever recorded, so he would retire him straight away he decided as he watched Dandy cross the line nearly 300 yards ahead. People would come for miles to his stud farm; Legacy would retire graciously, the most famous gypsy racer in history.

Tom was in utter shock as Dandy pulled to a steady slow trot, and looking around he saw Legacy far behind. He burst into a sob. "Thank you, thank you, son!" he cried.

Tom O'Donnell came straight over to Tom, pulling Legacy right up next to his sulky, his hand outstretched in respect. "Great race, Tom, well done. What an animal. Is he for sale?" he asked.

"Thank you, yes it was, and no he's not for sale," he replied, tears still tumbling down his big soft Irish face.

"Be careful now, Tom, you know they'll be after him." He winked and nodded, as he turned Legacy around and disappeared into the crowd.

The massive crowd engulfed them both, just wanting to touch Dandy and shake Tom's hand in recognition of one of the greatest races they had ever seen. Reagan who was stood with Daisy at the vantage point was also in tears. He had been watching, screaming out at the top of his voice, telling Daisy what was happening, but Daisy wasn't fazed, she knew he would win, he had told her so. Reagan returned to Jenny who was tied up to the large chestnut tree, and who was herself wondering what all the noise was about.

"Sorry, girl," he said as he tied Daisy back up, waiting for Tom to arrive. He had already packed everything ready for a quick escape and the sound of excited voices told him that Tom had returned. When he looked at his friend he saw that the look on his face said it all. A large crowd had followed Tom back to the little clearing where he and Reagan had made base.

Tom was clutching two bundles of money, five hundred pounds for him, and seven hundred and fifty for Reagan. The excited bookie had caught up with Tom and as promised, had paid him immediately, but all was not well on the course. Now every cider fuelled reveller and punter who had again just lost another packet, this time on Legacy, was very unhappy, and a mass brawl had started at the finish line, just outside one of the rough cider tents. The next thing everyone knew, the Garda had been called.

"Time to get out of here," Tom told Reagan, who had just finished packing the Sunday cart, quickly hitching Jenny to the sulky, and Dandy to the Sunday cart. Daisy would follow tied behind, much to her annoyance. "Sorry, girl, but we need to keep Dandy safe!" he told her.

"Okay, Master Tom," she replied.

"You can pull the cart tomorrow," he replied, satiating her. Packing and tacking quickly, the duo pulled out of the field. "Quick trot, Reagan," Tom shouted; they needed to be away fast. The two carts sped along the road into Gory, finally turning left to take the long road that led home. "See you at the fair tomorrow!" Tom called, raising his hand up in the air as Reagan banked right to go to his cottage.

A plume of smoke rising from the chimney stack told Tom that Reagan's wife, Claire was already cooking supper. The light was now fading, so Tom urged Dandy on towards home. Above the tall pines they trotted past, the sky was a mulitcoloured carpet of oranges, yellows and greys.

Christ he's not even tired, Tom thought to himself. "You okay, Daisy?" he whispered.

"Okay, Master Tom," she replied.

He smiled as serenity came over his being, a calmness he had never known and a deep inner peace enveloped him for the first time in his life. With just Reagan and the animals for company all day, he had been free of pressure, free of worrying about Patsy, the demon, his mother and of course his beautiful children. He sensed his father, Miles was there with him today, watching him, releasing all his worries, proudly watching him bring Dandy home safely, just as he had asked, doing the very thing he believed he was born to do. Until now he had not been able to follow his dreams, but now there were these two amazing God given beasts that were a big part of his and his mother's life, both of whom were born to work and race. They were beautiful animals with loving hearts bigger than a football.

Where would we be without them? he wondered.

Hearing Dandy turn the cart into the long stony lane, which led to the cottage, his thoughts were dragged back to the here and now.

"Oh, dear God, good lad, steady now!" he called to Dandy, but he knew the way, pulling steadily in through the gate and stopping right outside the cottage door, just as Daisy had shown him.

Margaret had sensed their arrival and came running out into the yard when she heard the sound of the stones crunching under the cart's tyres, relief showing on her craggy face on seeing both animals returned fit and well. Megan and Trixie also came running out of the cottage. Screams of delight filled the air, as hugs and kisses were given to both Daisy and Dandy who loved every moment of the attention. They helped unhitch them both and took them to the field gate.

A large pot of rainwater was warming over the fire pit and two fully filled oil lamps burned brightly either side of the cottage door. The smell of the beef roasting made Tom smile, suddenly realising that apart from the cider shandy Reagan had bought him, he hadn't consumed anything all day. His senses rebounded and came alive again as he emerged from the fog and warm blanket that had enveloped him all day. Once more he was alert to danger.

Working quickly, the Sunday cart was emptied and both Daisy and Dandy washed down, and dried with bunches of straw, then the lovely duo was released into the paddock, where they rolled and rolled in their favourite dust pit.

Margaret smiled as she watched them play before eventually tucking into the grass. "Well?" she enquired of him, a very tart tone to her voice telling Tom that she was unhappy with him.

"We have been racing."

"Yes I know, and I had to find it out from bloody Noleen at the shop. Why didn't you tell me? You could have put us all in danger?" she asked, bitterly.

"Don't fret, Mam. Do you honestly think I would let anything happen to either of these two?"

"It's not you, son, it's those bloody gypsies."

"I know, Mam. Don't worry. Dandy beat Legacy," he quietly told her.

"What?" she screamed in sheer disbelief.

"On Monday we are going down to the council office and I'm buying this cottage, so there will be no more rent to worry about, okay?" he said, smiling and turning towards her.

"Oh, son how?"

"I bet my last one hundred pounds on Dandy to win, and he did, and I got a good price, so, Mam, no more worrying, okay?"

"What about, Daisy?" she asked looking down to the floor unable to look at him, curiosity getting the better of her.

"Drew with The General."

"Drew! She should have won."

"Yes, she would have beaten the pants off him if she hadn't got excited and broken into a canter. I had to circle her, it's the rules. He was away by 500 yards, and she just ran out of track to pass him. Great race though."

"Oh my beautiful good girl." Margaret shook her head in amazement, and a little tear came in the corner of her old blue eyes with pride. "Supper's ready," she told him, and returned inside, calling the two girls who were still at the field gate and scratching both Daisy and Dandy under the chin.

Chapter 17

The demon strikes

HIS HIGH HAD ALMOST GONE by the time everything was cleaned, tidied and put away. Tom led Daisy and Dandy to the stable. Whilst tied to the field gate they had already consumed a feast of chopped kale, carrots and warm mash, which Tom had prepared earlier. A large vat of crisp rainwater was waiting for them to wash it all down. Sprinkling both with holy water, and thanking them for all their hard work today, both animals went quiet, and looked up at this gentle, man-mountain, both whickering, making Tom realise just how precious they were, and how lucky his family was to have them in their lives.

Saying goodnight he locked the door, started the exor chant, and started to bless the whole farm, sprinkling the holy water everywhere, much to the annoyance and frustration of the watching demon. Tom stopped sprinkling the holy water and chanting when he got to the field gate, distracted by the sight of the wheat, which was growing fast, swaying and ripening in the warm evening breeze.

Be a good harvest this year, he thought to himself standing quietly, relaxing, and trying to clear his head. From nowhere, and totally unexpected, a massive claw grabbed him around the neck from behind.

Cursing his stupidity he realised that he had left a little space unblessed, and for that one silly moment, the demon had seen his chance, and taken it!

THE DEMON'S GRIP WAS UNBELIEVABLE, and Tom struggled to breathe, his chest solid, almost as if he were in a cast iron straight jacket. Warm rivulets of blood trickled down his neck. The demon had caught him off guard in a little unprotected patch by the gate, no holy water on it or himself.

"Got you!" the demon cried out in triumph.

Tom, realising the strength of this evil being, suddenly understood in one split second what his wife Patsy had to deal with on a daily basis. He could feel himself being lifted off the ground and couldn't move; he was totally paralysed.

"Mam!" he called out in his head.

Margaret reacted instantly, fear and intuition sending a bolt through her and she immediately poked her head out of the door. At that very moment she saw her son Tom being attacked by an evil black being, which was trying to rise into the air with her son's limp body. She could see that Tom was totally lifeless, unable to move, and this sent her into a rage. Margaret rarely got violently angry, and always tried to keep calm, although her angry bouts were well-known and talked about. This is where Tom got his temper from, after all. Picking up a bottle of holy water and a broom, she charged into the well-lit yard.

"Bastard evil being, be gone!" she screamed, throwing the contents of the bottle over the back of the now frantically struggling demon, who instantly let Tom drop to the ground, the demon's screams filling the air as the holy water burned him.

Megan and Trixie ran into the yard on hearing the commotion outside, screaming and running to their father who lay hurt and prostrate on the floor. The evil black being was now starting to confront a wildly animated Margaret, and fear filled both girls, Trixie now screaming at the top of her voice.

Tom suddenly came to, drew in a large breath and saw the carnage being played out before his eyes. “Get back inside!” he ordered them.

Trixie didn’t think twice, turned and ran, but Megan thought otherwise. She grabbed two more bottles of holy water from the stash by the front door, and ran towards Margaret, dropping her fangs as she went, releasing her own demon. A confrontation now began. The black demon had Margaret trapped against the hedge, whilst Tom was getting to his knees but he was in an unprotected spot, and the demon knew it.

“Leave her!” Megan demanded as she slowly approached, her eyes totally focused on the demon.

Margaret winced when she saw Megan in full demon; it was quite a surreal moment, not frightening for anybody at all who was witnessing this paranormal scene.

“My beauty!” The black demon instantly pulled away from Margaret, letting her run to Tom, who was now standing and gazing in complete amazement at the scene unfolding in front of him. Clutching Margaret, they watched Megan stand in front of the evil being.

“Leave us!” Megan ordered the demon.

The demon stood motionless, licking his lips, raising his nose, smelling her alluring scent, his first bleed, his sacred and special one, the one he would die for so alluring was she.

“Come to me, my lovely,” called the demon. He held his hand out to her, long golden talons twisting, tickling the air towards him, gesturing for her to go to him.

“No!” screamed Tom and Margaret.

“Come with me, my lovely.” He beckoned to her again, golden drops of saliva falling from his fangs as the irresistible scent of this first bleed seduced him into a dreamlike state of erotic satiation. He leaned his head forward to sniff her.

Two angels suddenly appeared next to Tom and Margaret waiting to intervene, but Megan had come back to the here and now. The demon had tried to weave his magic spell, seducing her into his mind, sending her on an erotic journey up into the stars and beyond, but she had resisted. She was strong, really strong. The two bottles of holy water that she was holding and squeezing hard broke his spell. He was so lost in his own little evil world of selfish, obscene, erotic gratification that he didn't even see the contents of the two bottles until they splashed onto his face, totally catching him off guard.

"You'll never get me!" she screamed at him.

His face was burning and smoking badly, and steam filled the air. The demon let out a blood curdling scream, one that Margaret decided there and then she would never forget, as she signed herself with the cross, as it lifted up into the darkening skies, howling and screaming with rage.

Tom ran to the cottage and told Trixie to stay inside, as he finished covering the rest of the farm with holy water, whilst at the same time shouting the exor chant, which you could have probably heard in Gory. At that point the archangels nodded to each other and left, as there was nothing there for them to do, it seemed that it was all under control.

Margaret grabbed Megan, who had retracted her demon and was back into normal mode, kissing and thanking her. "God, he caught me out that time, but the bastard won't do that again," she vowed, as she started to bank up the fire pit, almost like a bonfire, which would burn bright all night.

Shocked and shaken, they sat and recited prayers of thanks and protection. The beef was delicious and tender, and melted in their hungry mouths, the potato cake was moist, and in the last hour of cooking, it was placed under the joint of beef so it absorbed all the delicious juices. Boiled and buttered kale, carrots and fresh garden peas, not forgetting the Yorkshire pudding, which nearly burst out of the fire box tin, made the meal complete. It was supposed to be a joyous celebratory meal to end a wonderful day, but everyone sat and ate in silence, suddenly realising the danger they had all been subjected to on a daily basis for all these years, understanding how hard it must be for Patsy.

Sleep came to them all that night, even the evil and protesting howl of the demon sat in the oak tree behind the cottage, which was harrowing to hear, didn't keep them awake. They were safe, tucked up in the cottage, warm and cosy in their beds.

They all knew that the demon would never give up, but he now had to totally rethink his plans of how to connect with his first bleed. He loved her great strength, she would bear him a strong son, the best son a demon could ever wish for, but there were still others around, sensing her, and he knew that he would have to fight again to keep her. The other worry for him was that he also knew that she knew she had badly wounded him and he needed to keep his strength up. He decided to leave and go and feed elsewhere to regain his strength. He knew that she would be safe for the moment with her father Tom, he would definitely see to that!

Bright and early the next morning, Tom and Margaret woke to the sound of Daisy and Dandy calling to be let out.

"Coming!" they both called out as they scrambled out of bed, trying to get to the stable as quickly as possible. When he unlocked the door Tom was still only dressed in trousers with no shirt or shoes. He made his way over to the animals calling their names as he went. It was a lovely warm May morning, the sun was already rising in the sky, and there wasn't a wispy cloud in sight, just a bright, beautiful, blue sky morning; it would be a lovely day. "Hello, my beauties," he greeted them as he unlocked the stable door.

Daisy, quickly followed by Dandy, pushed their way past him going directly to the field gate. The sight of the two animals frolicking and playing, chasing each other around the field, and then rolling in the sand pit, before finally settling to the very important job of tearing into the lush, abundant, grass and filling their hungry bellies, always made

Tom feel emotional. His emotions were already running riot after the events of the previous night, which had shaken him and everyone else to the core. Looking around the farm, he sensed no demon, and wondered perhaps whether the confrontation with Megan the previous evening, would give them all some respite from that evil being. He certainly hoped so. Today was a family day, a celebration of folk from all over the county gathering together, and one his mother always loved attending. God only knew how much longer he would have with her. Losing his father had been a terrible shock, and he was determined to make whatever life his dear mother had left as meaningful and as easy as possible. Today he had the joy and satisfaction of knowing that he could safely leave her in Ireland and return to England, without her having to ever again worry about paying the rent, because tomorrow he was buying the house for her from the council.

He now felt that he could relax. With breakfast over and all the animals seen to and fed, and the chores done, out again came the lovely shiny Sunday cart. Daisy was called from the field and given a nice brush down, dancing on the spot in anticipation of pulling the cart today. Tom would leave Dandy in the stable he decided, as he filled the two outside lamps with oil. He also filled the fire pit with wood for when they would return later in the early evening.

Ham hocks were put on to slowly cook while they were out. Onions and carrots, along with a leek and some thyme were all placed in the firebox which sat at the side of the slabs of peat that were smouldering slowly in the hearth. This acted like a slow cooker, and nothing ever burnt, so slow was the release of heat. The smell of the succulent meat in the broth would certainly welcome them all home later that day.

Chapter 18

May Day Fayre

DAISY TOOK THEM TO THE fayre in fine style, trotting with high legs, trying as always to show off her new shiny shoes. Megan and Trixie had never been to the May Day fayre before and when they arrived Tom whistled at the sight before him; it seemed even bigger than he could ever remember. The ploughing match was now in full swing in the field they had raced in yesterday, and the fayre was humming along nicely, full of excited families and revellers. The cider tents were bursting at the seams and a large Ferris wheel took centre stage along with all the stalls bulging with home-made goodies, houseware and bric-a-brac. Margaret especially was desperate to get shopping. They tied up in the field allocated for the animals pulling carts.

Spying Harry and Arkel further on in the line, Daisy whickered hello, which was immediately responded to. Settling her down with a hay net and water, and a hat to keep off the sun, the party headed towards the happy, noisy venue.

The hog roasts did brisk business and the hay bales which acted as seats were all taken by tired revellers. A cold shiver ran down Tom's spine, as he recalled when Patsy was with child, and Tinker just a small yearling, attending the show, him ploughing, Patsy meeting the gypsy who foretold the problems with the demon, and here he was now, with his mother and two beautiful girls, but as always, he sensed trouble.

"Tom!" came a cry from the crowd. It was Reagan. "We need to talk."

Tom told him, "Meet me in the race field where the ploughing match is, I'll be watching Kimmeridge's shire, top left hand corner, say in 15 minutes, okay?"

"Okay," replied Reagan. He receded back into the immense crowd disappearing as quickly as he had appeared.

Tom caught up with Margaret and told her he was heading for the ploughing match. She was already buying jams and marmalades, totally engrossed in the heaving stalls of produce that was for sale that lay ahead in the distance.

"Okay, don't be too long," she replied, telling Megan and Trixie to stay close as they made their way through the crowded market.

Reagan was already waiting at the top corner of the ploughing field when Tom arrived. "Hi, Tom, how are the beasts today?"

"You would never know that they had raced," he replied with a little smile on his face.

"Tom I've got something else to confess, I've mated Dandy to Jenny my little filly. Sorry, Tom, I couldn't help myself, I love the animal. Christ, did you see how he ran yesterday, he beat the shite out of Legacy, he couldn't touch him?"

"Oh, Reagan you really are a stupid bastard, you are leaving us wide open. The word already out is that the gypsies want him. I was offered one thousand guineas by O'Donnell after I beat him."

"Sorry, Tom."

"Look, Reagan we are going to have to dye him and keep him off the roads at the moment. Come over tomorrow with some sheep dye, say after two o'clock. I am taking Mam into town in the morning to the council, I am buying her cottage for her, it's the least I can do," he told him.

"Is it really that serious?" Reagan asked him, nervously.

“Yes,” replied Tom, “and if they can’t have him they will kill him, and any offspring.”

“Oh shite! Good God in heaven, what have I done?”

“Right, Reagan let’s try and put this mess right, see you tomorrow afternoon.”

“I’ll be there, Tom,” said the now worried blacksmith walking away to collect Star and to make his way home. He continually looked around now, an uneasy feeling creeping into his stomach, just in case he was being watched or even followed before reaching the safety of home.

The rest of the day was enjoyable. People stopped Tom, shaking his hand, congratulating him on the wonderful race and the fantastic win over Legacy, asking excitedly when he would be running again, the disappointment instantly appearing on their faces when he replied that he wasn’t sure, knowing that he could never race again, as it was far too dangerous. The other worry spinning around in Tom’s head was that if this ever got back to Legend’s owner, they would take Dandy away, and have him up in court, of that he was sure.

“Stupid greedy Reagan,” he cursed and shook his head, but what was done was done, and if he was living here with his mother he probably would have done the same. But Dandy’s life was now in danger his senses told him so, and he was listening carefully to them. He also knew that the gypsies would not stop until they found him.

THE REST OF THE DAY flew by. Four o’clock soon came and Tom knew it was time to leave. Margaret had shopped till she dropped, literally, buying all sorts of goodies, relishes, and a lovely chunky hand-knitted shawl, which she would use in the winter. She had also bought plenty of store goods, a new skirt, and some fresh looking cotton tea towels, not forgetting ribbons and hair clasps for the two girls. They in turn had feasted on hot dogs, jacket potatoes and lemonade, whilst Margaret had indulged in a ginger beer. Megan and Trixie had also been on all the fairground rides on offer. It certainly had been a lovely happy day, one that both girls would love telling their brothers about when they got home to England.

The weary family travelled home in a happy state, memories of the previous evening far away. Margaret was now thinking about the evening meal and had even splashed out and bought a loaf of Mary O'Rourke's famous soda bread as a treat for them all.

As soon as they were home the oil lamps were lit, bringing safe warm light into the darkening night that was creeping up on them. The cooking hams smelled appetising. Dandy was let out into the field to join Daisy who was already rolling in the dust pit. A serene sense of peacefulness cocooned them as they finished off their meal, and settled in for the night. The demon was nowhere to be seen or sensed, and the family for once, slept knowing they and their animals were all safe.

Chapter 19

The rent office

MARGARET AND TOM TIED DAISY up outside the rent office, and told Megan and Trixie to stay on the cart and look after Daisy while they attended to business inside. It was a grey still morning, and they had set off after all the chores were finished around the little farm, heading for Gory. First stop was the post office, then the large store *O'Reagan's*, and then the last item on the list was the rent office.

The rent office was bulging full of people, and there wasn't a spare chair anywhere. Most were attending to pay their monthly rent, some to complain about the long wait to get into council housing, whilst others were asking for repairs to their crumbling homes; it was a mismatch of happy and grumbling people. Council housing was in very short supply, and if you were lucky enough to get into one of the houses to rent you would move heaven and earth to keep it.

The muffled stamp bashing the paper of the rent book, echoed through the room. Margaret eventually found a chair, when someone was called up to the counter. She sat in the waiting area feeling a little queasy, not sure if it was worry or excitement welling up in her. Tom in the meanwhile was in the queue for the customer service counter with the others. His turn soon came.

"Hello, Mr Murphy, how are you and Margaret today?" enquired Annie McGuire, the normal customer service manager, feeling a little tingle go up her spine as she looked into this handsome man's face. She had always liked Tom and had met him out quite a few times at weddings and gatherings, but he never seemed to notice her. Obviously he only had eyes for his blonde haired wife. She had been so grieved when she had heard that he had married, as it seemed that another good one had got away.

"Fine thank you, Annie and yourself?" Tom replied realising that this little Annie, as he always knew her, had now become a woman and a very fine one at that. A little shiver flew through him.

"Yes, yes nothing to report at this end," she said, taking the rent money from the book, writing the date and amount carefully on the allotted line, and then bashing it hard with the official inked council stamp.

"Is Mr McCormack available for a quick chat?" Tom enquired.

"Why I think he is, Tom," she smiled, suddenly thinking how handsome he was, and how she would love to get to know him better, which instantly made her have a little flutter of a flush. She turned away in embarrassment fanning her face with a piece of paper. "Have a seat and I'll go and get him for you," she replied, heading towards his office, glad to be away from the counter and all the other customers who just might work out why she was flushing after who she had been talking to.

"Tom Murphy!" came the call. Tom and Margaret alighted and were greeted by a short, plump, little man with thinning ginger hair, a large smile and small round glasses. "Come in, come in please." He beckoned them towards his office, offering them both a comfy seat in front of his massive oak desk. "Well, Mr Murphy, Margaret, what can I do for you both, there are no rent arrears to worry about, or repairs pending, I have checked everything very thoroughly?" he was telling them as Tom cut in, not meaning to be rude.

"Oh no, Mr McCormack, it's nothing like that. Could you please tell us if we could buy Mam's cottage, and if so, how much would it be?" he enquired in earnest. Margaret was fidgeting in her chair, embarrassed, and not really believing she was in this conversation.

"Well, Mr Murphy, what a question. Can you afford it?" he queried back, not looking up, and being quite intimidating, shuffling papers on his desk and leafing through council files as he waited for the reply.

"I asked you, sir, if it was for sale and how much it would be, then I could answer you," Tom replied. Tom and Margaret went quiet.

Margaret now felt physically sick, feeling stupid, awash with shame. "Oh come on, son let's not waste our time here."

Mr McCormack continued to shuffle the papers on his desk. Margaret was ready to up and go, but Tom stayed and looked at this council official, waiting for the reply, a stern look in his eye telling McCormack to hurry up and make a decision, his hands tightening into fists.

"Mr Murphy, I didn't say it was not for sale, I just need to work out how much it's worth and what the council would sell it for. After all, you are indeed entitled to buy it, nearly 30 years of occupancy and no complaints makes for a good tenant, and of course, we would be losing that income, which has to be replaced." He spoke quietly, still not looking at them.

Margaret stood up. "Well?"

"Two years ago it was priced at two hundred pounds," said Tom.

"Yes, Mr Murphy that's correct, but land prices have risen and I need to take everything into consideration.

"We've no mains sewer, or electric, or gas, just a stand pipe," Tom replied.

"Oh really? Let's see what this comes to then. Have you asked your bank for a loan or mortgage?" he enquired. "I am afraid Mrs Murphy would not qualify for a council mortgage because of her age," he added, still not looking up at the now frustrated pair, Margaret wanting to bash him over the head with her basket at this moment in time, and Tom now telling her in his head to keep calm and let him handle it.

"For God's sake, man, will you please answer my question, how much will it cost?" Tom asked in a raised voice, which could be heard out in the waiting room.

Annie McGuire looked around at the other council employees mouthing to them, "What's all that about?"

"Sorry, right, Mr Murphy, four hundred pounds," McCormack replied, now flushing red from his neck to the top of his head, as embarrassment flooded him.

"That's double what it was, you thieving bastards!" Tom replied back.

"Yes I know, Mr Murphy, but it is prime land, and just under three acres, two point seven in fact, and I have a hundred people waiting to purchase this plot of land, should I wish to put it on the open market, and the cottage as well remember!" he pointed out.

But Tom knew that the council had just sold a cottage not far away, in a better position, with much more land, and the council had only charged Rory O'Brien three hundred pounds.

They must have heard about the race win, thought Tom. "Okay, we'll take it," Tom replied quietly and firmly.

"Yes! But, Mr Murphy, how are you going to pay for it?" McCormack asked again and getting exasperated.

"Oh, Tom I'll never get a bank loan, let's go, son, stop wasting your time with these egits," Margaret cried in despair.

"Shush, Mam!" Tom told her firmly. "Cash, Mr McCormack, cash," he said producing a massive wad of money from the inside pocket of his coat.

Mr McCormack nearly fainted on the spot; so it was true what he had heard about his horse beating Legacy. "There's also a fifty pound solicitor's fee to be paid in advance as well," he told him, gulping, his throat dry at the sight of all that money now laid out in front of him on the table. "Oh, there's also 5 years' council tax to be paid in advance, so the total is now five hundred pounds!"

"Five hundred pounds!" screamed Margaret, still in shock at the sight of all that money.

"Yes, Mr Murphy, the council requires five hundred pounds to complete this conveyance of land to you."

"Not to me, Mr McCormack, the house and land are to be conveyed to my mother, Margaret Murphy." Margaret was now in a complete state of shock, worry spreading all through her. "It's all there," said Tom pointing at the pile of cash now in neat rows on his desk. Margaret nearly swooned at the sight of all that money piled up in front of her on the desk.

"I want a receipt and the papers – today!" Tom told him.

"Mr Murphy, this usually takes weeks," he replied, beads of sweat rolling down on to his collar from his shiny perspiring head. The council was in turmoil and needed every penny. Five hundred pounds was a massive amount, would help refill the coffers and build even more houses for the homeless and needy, and there were plenty of them in Gory.

Tom laid another twenty pounds on the table. "Would this help speed things along? I leave for England at six o'clock tomorrow, and I want the papers delivered to the cottage before I leave."

Mr McCormack let out a big sigh. "Very well, Mr Murphy, I have some papers for you to sign," he said unfolding a large bill of sale land registry form.

"Oh no, not me, Mam it's your house," he said looking at her with pride. Margaret in the meantime was sat totally shocked and speechless.

"Well, Mrs Murphy? May I call you Margaret?" he nodded. "Please sign here, here, here and oh yes, here." He pointed at the spaces on the large legal paper, which she duly did, then he countersigned it, stamped it with an official council seal, and then produced another. "Please sign again in exactly the same places. This one goes to the Land Registry; the original will be signed by the Chief Councillor and delivered to you by six o'clock tomorrow."

"Receipt please!" added Tom.

"Oh yes, of course, wait one moment. Annie!" he called. "Please make out a receipt for five hundred and twenty pounds for Margaret Murphy."

"Five hundred and twenty pounds?" she asked back in shock.

"Yes, five hundred and twenty pounds, she has just purchased her house with cash!"

"How can that be?" she called back in sheer disbelief.

"The race the other day, it must be true, he beat Legacy."

"Oh my, oh my," she commented, filling out an official council receipt and witnessing the received amount for Mr McCormack to sign and officially seal.

Once done, the gossip quickly spread around the small office and Margaret and Tom proudly walked out towards Daisy and the girls. Tom turned and thanked the office girls, praying and thanking the Lord that he had had enough to pay for it. Margaret was also praying, feeling grateful, and at last, for the first time in her life, she was financially secure.

They called back into Gory on the way home. Margaret had made an excuse that she had forgotten lard and sugar and needed to pop back into *O'Reagan's*. While they were shopping and browsing at the same time, Margaret spied Noleen walking around, generally keeping an eye on things, and chatting to the customers.

"Noleen!" Margaret called to her.

"Ah, Margaret, good day to you. What can I do for you?" she asked earnestly.

"Do you sell radios?" she asked her excitedly.

"Why yes we do, they are over there on the back wall next to the last till," she told Margaret pointing in the general direction of where she would be headed.

Margaret quickly called out to the girls, who were looking at the meat counter, and they instantly came running to her side, but Tom had already beaten her to it. He knew she had wanted a radio for some time, and the leftover winnings still sat in his pocket. Ten pounds was an awful lot of money for a small brown contraption with a large round dial, and a leather carry strap, but it would make his mother's life more comfortable, and definitely less lonely, and so it was purchased. Margaret emerged from *O'Reagan's* with her lard and sugar, and a very nice, brand new, top of the range, modern transistor radio.

On their return to the farm, Reagan had already arrived. Star was tied to the entrance gate, hitched up to the small racing sulky.

"Tom; Margaret," he acknowledged them as they arrived.

"What in God's name is he doing to Dandy?" Margaret screamed in alarm.

Reagan had Dandy tied to the field gate, quietly chewing on a half-eaten hay net while he was attending to him. He had dyed half of Dandy black already; it was such a shock.

"Don't fret, Mam, I asked him to do it, it'll keep him safe," he told her.

Megan and Trixie screamed out with delight, running over to see him.

"Don't touch him he's still wet," Reagan told the two giggling girls as they ran towards him.

Tom was helping with the shopping, and a little smile came over Reagan's face as he saw him take the large brown box with *Phillips* on the side in big bold letters, into the cottage.

Margaret in the meantime was in a real strop. Tom was getting a little annoyed and she was completely ignoring him as he carried the bags in and placed them on the table.

"Mam?"

"What?" she replied sharply, her tone scathing and curt.

"Dandy won a race that has bought you your home and a bloody radio!"

She stopped for a moment and gathered her thoughts. "Oh sorry, son, forgive me, it's just that – all this change," she mumbled, now feeling very silly and ungrateful.

"I know, Mam, but don't worry, it'll be fine," he told her as they busied around the cottage lighting the fire and starting on the evening meal.

Two hours later, Dandy was put back into the field. He was now jet black with a large white star on his forehead, and four white socks, and his mane was hogged; he looked a totally different animal. Tom thanked Reagan reminding him he was leaving for the ferry the next evening.

"I'll call around before ye go," Reagan told him, smiling as he gathered Star together, and quietly making his way down the long stony lane towards home.

It was another warm May evening, and the distant sound of the radio from inside the cottage made Tom smile as he once again blessed the whole of the farm, sprinkling holy water all around. He had found and repaired an old water spray in the back of the barn. Filling it with holy water he was able now to spray the top of the cottage and even some of the branches of the oak tree. The fire pit was burning bright, so were the two oil lamps, but tonight, again, he did not sense the demon. Perhaps this would be a respite? He would always be on his guard. He touched the deep red scratches around his throat and thought of Patsy and the two boys. He prayed for a safe journey home, protection for them all, and some kind of contact from his dear friend Thomas Jones.

Chapter 20

Naughty Reagan

It had been 12 months since Dandy had beaten Legacy, and both Ellie and Brendan's hinnies had given birth to lovely foals, one a colt the other a pretty filly. As promised, they had paid two hundred pounds to Reagan, and he in turn, as agreed, gave it to Margaret, just as Tom had instructed. Reagan's lovely Jenny had also given birth to a beautiful filly that had all of Dandy's markings, and she would look just like her father in later years. Reagan was slightly disappointed it wasn't a colt, but she was a little beauty, and he decided to call her Poppy.

All was well with Reagan. Claire had produced a little girl and she was christened Mary after his mother and little Tommy was doing really well at school. The café had become a complete success, just as Reagan had predicted, becoming a regular hang out for the locals. Claire was astute enough to now sell cider and beer which went down especially well with the menfolk who regularly gathered at the farm, watching Reagan toil away, whether they had an animal with them or not; yes everything in life was good. Reagan should have been content yet still he had a yearning to race Dandy again, despite Tom's warnings. A new local fayre would soon be due and the gypsies would once again be coming to town to race, right next to the hundred acre field.

Dandy was still black, with four white socks and a white star in the middle of his face between his eyes. His tail and mane had become shaggy and long. Margaret was doing her best to keep them up together, but their unkemptness would work in his favour again, as he did not look anything like the animal that beat Legacy.

Margaret's health was ailing, arthritis was setting in, and her old bones especially her spine, were becoming painful. Her joints were swollen and inflamed, but the worse thing was her forgetfulness which seemed to be getting worse on a daily basis.

Tom had phoned Reagan only a week ago, asking him to drop by, as she had not replied to his last letter. Reagan of course immediately agreed, now hatching a plan to take Dandy to train secretly, on the pretence of keeping him fit, so as not to waste away being unused.

The very next day he set out for Margaret's in his van. He beeped the horn as he pulled into the yard and Margaret immediately came out into the yard. This was her signal that people were arriving and she was very pleased to see Reagan.

"How are you, Margaret?" he asked her.

"Oh fine, fine," she replied.

"Have you been to town this week?" he asked her.

"No, oh, at least I don't think so," she replied, feeling slightly confused.

"Well I can take you, Margaret, Tom phoned last evening, asking me to call in and work Daisy and Dandy so they don't get bored," he told her.

"Oh, thank you."

"Margaret, Tom tells me you haven't replied to his last letter."

"Oh Lord in heaven, then no I haven't been to town, it's still sat on the shelf," she replied sheepishly.

"Right then, I'll get Daisy harnessed up and we'll have a nice ride into town," he told her.

Margaret excitedly changed and gathered together her bag and bits for the journey, taking the letter down off the shelf.

"Do you have a list, Margaret?" Reagan called to her. Tom had asked Reagan to make sure she had a list as her mind was now starting to wander.

"Oh no, wait! I'll do one now," she told him scuttling back inside and scribbling down all the essentials she needed.

Daisy danced and pranced all the way into Gory and back again. With all the shopping done Margaret invited Reagan in for a cup of tea.

"It's okay, Margaret, I'll take Dandy out for a trot just like Tom asked me to, I'll have one when I get back," he sheepishly replied, quickly tacking Dandy up to the Sunday cart, and watching with a smile as Daisy frolicked in the dust pit.

Reagan took Dandy down to the hundred acre field, and set about walking him around the field one way, changing to the other way, four times, just as Tom had instructed him before. Dandy knew exactly where he was and quickly picked up pace.

"Steady, lad," Reagan told him. He could feel the power of this beast just waiting to be unleashed as he pulled him back.

One hour later he arrived back at Margaret's with a huge smile on his face. The races were in 6 weeks' time, and Reagan knew, even though he only had 6 weeks, it would be enough to get some sort of race fitness into him. Dandy was still so fast, he would ace his race. Daisy in the meantime started to get agitated, whickering and calling at the gate every day when Reagan called to take Dandy out. She knew that he was training to race and she wanted to race as well. Why wasn't she going?" Torment was now getting the better of her, so much so that Margaret had to come out and placate her, always telling her Dandy would not be long and that she would be next, but of course that never happened.

Realising that Daisy was fretting, and so as not to arouse suspicion, Reagan made a point of taking Margaret into town twice a week, always pushing Daisy hard on the way back, telling Margaret that Tom had told him to do so, to make sure they both didn't get lazy or bored. Margaret didn't mind, she was in heaven, only too glad of the company and the lovely trips into town, so lonely had she become now.

Race day finally came around. It was a much smaller affair than the last one with just a handful of gypsies from Cork, two bookies, one cider tent and about three to four hundred racegoers milling around the start/finish line.

Reagan was in the first race, and he had registered himself and 'Rocky' to race. They were up against a very good chestnut filly called Cherry. At 15 hands she was a stoutly built girl who had won her last three races, up against very good horses. Reagan had crept into Margaret's yard very early that morning. He had let Daisy out into the field, unhitched Star to keep Daisy company, given them both a warm juicy apple, and then left them frolicking and playing in the paddock. Dandy had been quickly hitched to the racing sulky and driven to the hundred acre field. He was so race fit that Reagan had believed he could drive Dandy to the fayre, race him and drive him home again all inside a couple of hours and that Margaret would never even know or suspect anything was amiss. Well that was his plan anyway.

DANDY TROTTED BEAUTIFULLY TO THE races, arriving with 30 minutes to spare. Reagan registered with the course steward and gave Dandy a quick rub down. First on, they were called to the start and the crowd was humming with anticipation. Reagan was nervous and feeling really sick. His hat felt damp, beads of perspiration dripped down his back, and his sweaty hands gripped the reins as the beautiful chestnut filly pulled up alongside them at the start. She was driven by a young lad called Shaun Flynn. He tipped his hat and smiled at Reagan and wished him good luck, which now had the instant effect of making him want to wretch.

The flag dropped, Reagan had missed it, his nerves getting the better of him and the filly was already way out in front, thick clods of earth going up into the air, as she ripped through the thick pasture. Reagan reacted to his mistake and pushed Dandy on. Dandy responded immediately, quickly catching the chestnut beauty and passing her just before the first bend and winning the race by miles, leaving her in his wake.

Silly Reagan, he had just made a fatal mistake. He passed the winning post, gently slowing and turning Dandy to go and shake hands with Shaun Flynn.

The young man stormed over to Reagan and immediately spat in his face. "What sort of horse do you have there: no ordinary one I bet, what are you hiding?" he asked him, pure venom pouring out of this embarrassed young man's face.

Other gypsies drew around the sparring pair, touching and inspecting Dandy from top to toe. He was hardly blowing and loved the race, and was now prancing and getting very animated, loving the attention. Reagan had betted the day before, passing over one hundred pounds in the *Royal Oak* to the bookies. This had instantly aroused suspicion; the word was that Reagan had helped Tom Murphy beat Legacy some time ago, with a 14.2 hands roan stallion; it was so fast that nobody had ever seen the like. It had broken the course record, led to Legacy's retirement, and then as suddenly as he had appeared, he had vanished.

Reagan was suddenly very frightened, realising what he had done. Oh God, how he wished that Tom was there now. He had let Dandy go, beating the pants off the opposition and making everyone suspicious that this was the horse that beat Legacy. He didn't even race, he should have kept hold of him and let him go 200 yards before the line, and make it look like a fair fight, but the gypsies didn't like being beaten especially when they suspected foul play.

The one hundred pound wager was thrown in his face, only to be taken by the wind, scattering it down the course, drunken revellers chasing the paper money, hoping to refuel at the cider tent with it.

A large burly man came over to Reagan and also spat in his face. "Fucking shyster!" he called to him, grabbing Dandy by the head.

Dandy immediately reared, sending this thick bully unceremoniously to the ground. Sensing something was wrong, Dandy pulled off instantly, with Reagan hanging on for dear life as Dandy fled, with the little sulky bumping around behind him.

Reagan realised that he was in very serious trouble, and so was Dandy, and it was his fault. He slowly gathered Dandy back under his control, soothing him from his fright back at the racecourse. He pushed on for home along the road to Gory and then his home, fretting and trying to work out what he was going to do to keep Dandy safe. Just before the turning into the lane which led to his cottage, he had a secret track, one he used when he wanted a short cut home. Stopping and nervously looking around to see if he was being followed, he pulled back a large shrub and bush, pushed Dandy through into the field, and told him to wait for him whilst he covered the entrance back over. You would have never known it was there. The track led to the back of his barn where he had a secret stall. He arrived puffed and very nervy, not knowing what to do, fear enveloped his whole being, and he started to shake.

"Stupid bastard, what have I done?" he cursed himself, crying with shame and looking at the glorious animal he had just let down, and badly. "Oh, Lord and Tom, please forgive a silly man," he cried out, as he untacked Dandy who was now back to his old self, laid back, and quite enjoying being in a different environment. He quickly made up the spacious stall, and gave Dandy plenty of food and water. He decided the safest thing to do was to keep him there tonight, and not even his wife Claire would know that he was there, it was the best thing all round. Once he was settled in, he saddled up Jenny who was at that time quietly grazing with her foal in the pasture. He rode like a madman to the farm where Margaret was hanging out the washing.

"Reagan, what ails, where's Dandy?" she asked, dropping the washing back into the basket and running over to him.

"Oh, Margaret, don't worry, he's at my farm, he picked up a stone in his hoof this morning, he's sore. I am waiting for a call from Tom, he'll tell me the best way to treat it," he lied, feeling absolutely terrible about doing it. "I'll have him back, but it might not be until the morning," he told her.

"Oh, Reagan, are you sure he's okay?" she asked, absolutely knowing something was up, but knowing she had to trust this man who had helped bring Dandy into the world, and who was now a large part of her life.

"Promise," he told her feeling anxious and suddenly feeling that he must get back to Dandy and making a plan in his head. He'd have to own up to Tom about what he'd done. He realised with great shame and embarrassment how stupid and greedy he had been. Not only had he put himself and Dandy in danger, but also his own bloody family.

What was I thinking? he questioned himself angrily.

He tied Jenny to the back of his cart and hitched up Star who really didn't want to leave Daisy. Not only were they kin, they were also good friends, and he had enjoyed her company today, but when Reagan came to collect him, he bade farewell to his sister, and duly went back to work.

Reagan pushed on for home, leaving Margaret fretting, wondering what the hell was the matter. She'd have to write a letter to Tom. She'd do it now, and she would put Daisy in her stable for safety.

Star was pushing on nicely, wondering what the matter was. He could feel the anxiousness in his master, and nervous energy flowed from his hands down the reins, making Star edgy. He strode out wanting to get Reagan home now as quickly as possible, but trouble was waiting just 500 yards before the turning to his cottage.

The races were over, the rest of the duels having been won by the visiting gypsies from Cork. The revellers had dispersed, most lacking money in their pockets, the bookies being the total winners today. But Shaun Flynn and his family had been embarrassed. They had a cracking horse, a winner, a good genuine one at that, but they had been upstaged by a fraudster and a cheat, and they were looking for revenge.

The van slowed and stopped right in front of Reagan, making him pull up sharply. Jenny objected from behind, almost running into the back of the cart, shrieking in surprise at the sudden stop. Flynn and two large burly Irishmen built like brick outhouses got out of the van and walked towards Reagan who was now nearly shitting himself.

"Bastard cheating, Reagan Callow!" Flynn spat nastily at him, in a sheer venomous and evil tone. At the same time he spat a large gob of spittle straight at him, this being the worst gypsy insult you could ever have, and when it comes, you are most definitely in danger. An arrow struck Reagan that very second, and for the first time in his life, he felt real fear.

"Where's the racer, who is he?" he asked, slapping a thick shillelagh in his hand menacingly. An evil smirk on his face told Reagan he meant business!

Reagan suddenly thought on his feet. *God and Lord above forgive me please!* he said in his head before he uttered his words. "Sorry, boys, I borrowed the beast, his owner has just been and collected him. I just wanted to have some fun, no harm meant," he replied, but his flushed face and worried look made him still seem suspicious to them.

"Where the fuck is he?" Flynn again asked menacingly, saying don't mess with me now or you are dead, I mean business. The other two men slapped their equally huge shillelaghs in their hands in a threatening manner.

Reagan gulped and whispered quietly, "He's on the other side of Gory, small farm, large red gates; you can't miss them, on the Kilmeaden road.

He had just told them about an honest and very good working horse he shoed every 6 weeks, but he was also used for racing and only won now and again. He belonged to a lovely couple called Molly and Aiden O'Brien. The horse was called Paddy, a lovely lad 5 years old, black, four white socks, and a star in the middle of his forehead. In fact, when Reagan was dyeing Dandy, this was the very horse he was thinking about.

Reagan shuddered as he spoke his words. "Oh feck! Oh shite! What have I done?" his soul cried inside, as the gruesome three looked at him.

Suddenly feeling he was telling the truth, they left him, got back into the van and drove away. Reagan was stunned and fear filled his whole being. He sat and waited for them to recede from view up the hill, before picking up the reins, and pushing on along the road for another 500 yards, then turning left into the lane that led to his cottage.

Chapter 21

Tom

TOM WAS NOW AT HOME with the children. Patsy was still under treatment in Barrow Gurney, so he had taken a job a lot closer to home in a factory not too far away in Brislington, making brake linings for cars. The money was average, but he worked it out as a family he could survive and he could look after the children and be at home every night where he needed to be.

He had given Reagan his next door neighbour's phone number. Her name was Audrey Collings, and this number was to be used for emergencies only. His neighbour was the road nosey, but also a willing and sexy cougar, a real man eater, eager for sex, men, flesh and whatever or whoever she could literally lay her hands on, and she most definitely had the highest hots for Tom. God only knew how many times he had had to fend her off. She was a sexy, good looking woman, who actually looked after herself, but with no children and no family near, she had become obsessed with men, and the lack of one in her life. She had nearly caused one young painter from the council to be sacked after keeping him hostage in her house for 3 days, having wonderful sex, realising that he had an amazing escape from this lady when his boss ordered his colleagues to come and rescue him.

Reagan's call came late that night. Audrey promised to relay the message.

Oh! Tom Murphy coming to use my telephone. Oh! She was already feeling faint, fantasising about how she would get him to her big brass bed this time. She had to make a plan, a good one and it was already in place by the time her little note dropped through Tom's letter box at three am that morning.

Tom picked up the note on the front doormat when he went downstairs to make breakfast. A sudden shudder went through him; trouble in Ireland again, but this time he felt danger and not from the demon. Real danger, perhaps for his mother, or Dandy, he didn't exactly know, but he knew it was bad trouble whenever he felt like this. Worse still, he would have to face the cougar next door. He needed her phone, this was an emergency, the red phone box down the road was out of use, and the nearest phone box was an hour's walk away. No, Audrey's phone next door it would have to be. He'd have to make a plan, a quick getaway if it was needed. He started to plan it in his head. Tonight would be the night. He took a deep breath, his head spinning, thinking about both problems as he went into the kitchen to light the oven, and cook breakfast.

Audrey was sat patiently waiting for Tom to knock on her door and ask to use her telephone. She had bathed, shaved her minge, armpits and legs, moisturised and applied a thick coat of make-up, put on false eyelashes, and the shortest of skirts with no panties. After a quick coiffure of her long dark hair, applying fresh lipstick, the darkest of red she could find, and putting on high-heeled shoes, and then squirting perfume in every possible place, she was finally ready, a hungry praying mantis waiting for its meal.

Yum, she thought. She actually hadn't had a man for a long time. Well, 12 months really, the last one had been that gorgeous young painter that the council had allocated to her house to paint her windows and doors. She had kept him longer than the 3 days he was scheduled, nearly wearing him out with her sexual demands. He was young and single and had taken the opportunity of having a brief sexual encounter with a good looking, well-kept, older woman. It could do no harm; she was single as well. But after 6 days, and hardly any work completed, and the project nearly finished, his boss, Fred Mathews, had assigned two other painters to help complete the job, realising that this cougar, the same one he had encountered, was probably the reason Billy Wright, a normally quick and very efficient worker, could not get this job done on time as planned.

Much to her annoyance, the threesome finished the job that very day, and as they walked down the garden path, the other two workmen laughed, telling Billy what a lucky boy he'd been, being able to have so much fun and sex while he was supposed to be working. Embarrassed at being found out, he knew he would have his leg pulled for some considerable time, and his new nickname became 'Billy the bonker' and one that would stick for as long as he worked for the council.

Megan had just finished the shepherd's pie, and the creamy leek and swede mash topping with cheese sprinkled over the top, sat waiting to be put into the oven. She had fried the leftover lamb from the Sunday lunch, sweating it down with onions, and garlic and a little tomato paste, before making lovely meaty mint sauce gravy to complete the magic of the meal. Fresh carrots, garden peas and fried cabbage with bacon and onion was a family favourite, and would not last long. She had made it just like her Granny Margaret and her mother had shown her. Two freshly cooked soda breads sat on the counter top cooling in the evening air.

"You okay, love?" Tom asked her.

"Fine, Dad, dinner in 30 minutes, is that enough time for you to make the call?" she asked him, knowing that trouble was brewing.

"I only need a couple of minutes, that's all I want to be in that house," he replied with an apprehensive look on his face.

"Good luck!" she called after him as he picked up a two shilling piece, and put it in his pocket to pay for the call.

Audrey had gotten herself into a right old tizzy. She was having this man tonight she had decided, and two very large glasses of white wine later, the scene was set. Her beautiful opulent bed was open, with cushions plumped and looked very inviting. Two wine glasses and another unopened bottle sat on the dressing table, waiting to be consumed. Candles were lit all around the house, giving it a soft, evocative glow. She had taken off her bra, her ample bosom spilling down in full view in the low-necked soft top. Her large, deep red, pert nipples were covered, but only just, standing to attention in excited anticipation of being stroked or even kissed, which no male with a normal sex drive could resist. She knew this and was banking on Tom being totally obsessed with her. Her skirt was very short, and her long slim legs were finished off with high heel shoes. She looked the very part she wanted to: irresistible. With no panties on, every stride revealed the thick curly dark hair of her bush, and to complete her seductive look, she wore lashings and lashings of dark red lipstick, her favourite, the colour men went mad for. She always knew this, it had always worked before, and it would work again tonight.

THE KNOCK CAME JUST AS expected, and Audrey opened the door and smiled.

"Hi, Audrey, may I use the phone please?" asked Tom gulping at the sight of this sex on legs cougar who was waiting to devour him.

"Why of course, Tom, please come in," her eyes widening excitedly on seeing this beautiful muscular man-mountain entering her house. She showed him the way to the telephone with her extended arm.

"Oh, Jesus, Mary and Joseph, give me strength," he whispered as he walked through the hall to the telephone.

"Whiskey, Tom? I've a Jameson's."

"Why thank you, Audrey," he replied nervously not even looking at her, taking a piece of paper out of his pocket, and setting it down on the shelf to dial the number.

Yes! she screamed inwardly whilst in the kitchen, shaking her arm in joy. She had him, it was the very first time he had ever acknowledged her kindness, and accepted the whiskey. God only knew how many times in the past he had refused it, but tonight he had said yes. She poured a very large glass of the smooth Irish whiskey, quickly finished off another large glass of white wine, and took a slug from another bottle she had opened in the fridge.

Her womanly yearn for sex was aching. Oh how she needed attention and she wanted it now. She dipped her fingers into the whiskey and rubbed it on her throbbing sex, hoping it would taste nice for Tom.

"Oh fucking hell!" she screamed out, running up the hallway, dumping the whiskey down next to Tom who was quietly speaking on the telephone, and going upstairs to the bathroom. Her bits were on fire.

What was I thinking? she wondered as she ran a cold tap and applied a cooling flannel to her now burning undercarriage. She sighed with the relief that the cold water brought.

She could hear raised voices downstairs, and once again her amour rose. "I have to have sex tonight!" she screamed, as she liberally applied Vaseline to her still throbbing bits. She was desperate to get back downstairs to that sexual god on her telephone in the hallway, but the whole bottle of wine she had consumed was now kicking in, and her head had started to spin, and suddenly she felt very sick.

On hearing the sound of violent retching coming from upstairs, Tom quickly made another call to the hospital where Patsy was staying.

"Oh at least another 3 weeks, Mr Murphy," came the information he needed from the sister in charge of the ward.

"Thank you, please tell my wife I will see her soon," he told her, quickly putting down the phone, throwing the whiskey into the rubber plant that stood next to the phone, and leaving the two shillings for the call. Then as fast as he could he exited the house, quietly closing the door behind him.

Audrey in the meantime had got herself into a state. "Coming, lover!" she called out in between each vomit, her head spinning like a top. She tried to get up from the toilet bowl, miscalculated her position, and whacked her head hard on the hand basin. She crumpled into a drunken heap onto the bathroom floor covered in her own stomach contents, and there she stayed until the morning.

Tom had had a lucky escape, or so he thought. Patsy though was sat in the corner of her little room at the hospital, her eyes glowing green, seeing everything!

Tom came in through the back door, the waft of the shepherd's pie drifting all around the little kitchen. Carrots and peas were sat cooked and steaming, and cabbage and bacon was frying on top of the stove.

"Nearly ready," said Megan. Trixie was laying the table. The two boys flew in through the door, a muddy football in their hands. "Wash up, dinner's ready!" shouted Megan after them as they alighted the stairs two at a time.

"Girls," said Tom quietly, "I have got to go to Ireland tomorrow."

"Oh, Dad, can we come?" Megan and Trixie instantly blurted out.

"No, sorry it's school for you. I'll be back in a week. I'll leave rent money and everything you need. Mam's okay and it will probably be about 3 weeks before she's out," he said feeling terrible that he could not take them with him. Margaret would have loved that, but with everything else going on, and Patsy still in hospital, he couldn't ask the neighbours to look after the boys, especially Audrey next door. God only knew what would happen. No, he knew in his heart that Megan could cope, and he would relax knowing she could look after the home and her siblings while he was away, and he needed to go now, well first thing in the morning.

The shepherd's pie was delicious and not a scrap of anything was left. The leftover rice pudding was put into the fridge, where it would firm, ready to slice and serve cold with a dollop of jam on the tea tray tomorrow. Tom made ready, packing his bag and talking to Megan while she was pressing the school uniforms for the morning. Sealing envelopes, money inside, marking on the outside what they were all for, he decided he would get the five o'clock bus to Temple Meads Station in the morning.

Chapter 22

A reckoning

REAGAN'S WIFE CLAIRE WAS VEXED at the anxious state Reagan had returned in. It was nine thirty at night, and he was still out in the stable.

"What are you doing?" she asked him entering the barn and seeing the soft glowing light at the back. She had a tray with some sliced boiled ham, boiled potatoes in the skins (poppies) all covered in a thick parsley sauce with a slice of soda bread, thickly buttered. "Oh, love!" she commented on seeing him next to a chestnut roan horse covered in grease and melted white candle wax, stuck in chunks in his tail and mane.

"Coming, coming," he nervously replied.

"Is that Tom and Margaret's horse?" she asked him, her face showing surprise.

"Shush, don't mention it to anyone, I have just taken all the dye off of him, you're to say nothing to anybody, and I mean no one!" he told her firmly. His tight squeeze on her arm alarmed her.

"Reagan please!"

"Look, Claire, the gypsies have found out that this was the horse that beat Legacy, and they are looking for him, and if they find him, they'll kill him, so promise me you'll say nothing to man or woman."

"Oh sorry, love, of course, my word is my bond, he looks awful!"

she commented. "Nah, he'll be fine tomorrow, just changing him, his markings, that's all," he told her.

He said goodnight to Dandy who was so in his own little world, nothing worried him, and he carried on munching a sweet hay net with not a care in the world. Reagan locked the door tight. He put Jenny, Star and the new hinny, Poppy into the paddock at the front of the house, and lit two large oil lamps which would burn all night and give plenty of light. Then he double padlocked the tall house gates and left his two hounds Rufus and Medley inside the front porch; they would howl and sound the alarm should anyone come around in the night. He sat in the kitchen nervously eating his supper which was now cold, but still tasted great. Gosh was Claire a good cook! He thanked the Lord for her being in his life, along with little Tommy and Mary, saying prayers of protection and apologising for the terrible mess and problems he had created through his own greed. He would have to go to confession now and get the priest to absolve him of his sins.

Heck, he shuddered; *it would probably be about one hundred Hail Mary's for this one.*

He was due to pick Tom up later tomorrow. He would drive to the ferry port at Rosslare and pick him up there, it was the least he could do. Tom was getting the day boat, which was nothing more than a converted cattle boat, which would dock at six pm the next evening.

The next day Reagan was waiting on the side of the little dock, as the old, rusty and battered white and green Irish Ferry slowly and gently manoeuvred into her berth. Within minutes the white metal gangplanks were placed against her hull, and tired and eager travellers began to disembark after gathering at the top of gangplanks waiting to be released onto the sacred earth, that was to them Ireland. Loved ones and friends also gathered around, and various trains sat in the little station at the side of the berth waiting to take loved ones and friends to their final destination. Reagan spied Tom immediately; how could you miss a man-mountain with a massive holdall on his shoulders, as he made his way down the slippery gangplank.

"Tom!" he called, waving his arm.

Tom acknowledged him immediately, and made his way through the throng of people to where he stood. "Reagan you sloppy bastard," he said, shaking his head and holding out his hand to shake his at the same time in real friendship.

"Oh, Tom I am so sorry," he replied, really meaning it and feeling quite ashamed.

"Well what's done is done, let's try and sort it out now," he told him.

It would be a steady hour and a half drive to Margaret's house. Reagan had made sure to inform her he was arriving today on the day boat and that he would pick him up from Rosslare and safely deliver him home.

"Well how did it go?" Tom asked Reagan, as they travelled along quiet, tree lined leafy roads.

"The dye came out exactly as you said and he looks like his old self now. I've left the boot polish on his coat, and the melted white candle wax in his mane and tail as you told me to. He'll be out in the dust pit tomorrow, and then we can sort him.

"Good, good," said Tom quietly. "Fancy a pint?" he asked him as they reached Gory. It would be good to let everyone know he was back; it might help quieten the situation.

Reagan parked outside the *Royal Oak*. The pub was heaving, a skittles match had just finished and plates of freshly made cheese and onion sandwiches were being passed around the bar to everyone present, and pints of the black stuff lined the bar.

"Reagan! Tom!" the barman Aiden Boyle called out acknowledging them both. "How are ye both?" He pushed two black and tan settled pints that were on the bar towards them.

Reagan immediately handed him a ten shilling note. "Keep the change!" he told him taking the two pints and joining Tom, who was sat on a high stool in the window at the front of the pub.

Before either of them could start a conversation, the bookie Miles O'Leary came over to them, slapping Tom on the back. "Tom, Reagan, how the devil are you?" he said extending his hand in friendship.

"Well, thank you and yourself?" Tom enquired back.

"Yes," Miles replied, "business is good. I hear you had a run in with Flynn, Reagan. He's mighty mad; they found Rocky, your racer, dead this morning with a slit throat and its hooves and ears missing. It looked just like the horse you raced at the weekend. Was it?" he asked him quietly.

Reagan suddenly felt sick, his face and neck reddened, and he wanted to suddenly sob. "Miles, for God's sake shut the fuck up and mind your own business," he reacted to him.

"Tom, sorry, no harm meant, I was only saying…" said Miles.

Tom cut him short. "And I'm saying as well."

"Okay, okay, just being friends and passing on a friendly warning, he's still after you, Reagan," O'Leary told him, turning away and walking back to the bar to join his friend.

Reagan burst into tears. "God, Tom, what have I done?"

"Quiet, friend if they've killed McConnell's colt, we might be okay. Don't worry, it would have been insured and killed quickly," he said looking deep into his half-drunk pint. "He'll be back though, we need to get Dandy back to Mam's farm. If he is still around and looking he'll have me to deal with."

The ride home to Margaret's was silent, both Tom and Reagan constantly looking around, keeping an eye out for anyone watching. Reagan left Tom at the bottom of the stony lane; there was enough moonlight to brighten the way. When he reached the gate, two oil lamps burned bright, one on each side of the cottage door. Daisy was standing at the gate, and the smell of cooked food wafted around the yard. Tom went straight to the field gate and gave Daisy the warm apple he had in his pocket for her. She whickered with delight.

"Shush now, girl, stay at the other end of the field tonight under the hedge, we want you out of sight. And keep quiet," he told her.

"Yes, Master Tom," she replied walking away and eventually cuddling up into the hedge at the end of the field, which instantly made her almost impossible to see.

He closed and locked the main gate, and quickly lit a fire in the fire pit.

"Is that you, Tom?" came Margaret's voice putting her head outside the door on hearing the gate clang shut.

"Mam, I'm banking up the fire pit!" he called to her.

"Where's Daisy?" she asked, worried.

"Oh don't worry about her, she's down the bottom of the field cuddled up to the hedge out of sight, just like I asked her to," he replied.

"Come on, son dinner's ready!" she told him, while he was taking stock, looking around the farm.

"Coming," he said, picking up his holdall, going inside and locking the door firmly behind him.

The next morning was bright and sunny and Daisy was stood at the field gate.

"Morning, girl!" he called.

She did her little excited dance on the spot in acknowledgement. The embers in the fire pit were glowing a soft orange. He stoked them and small flames burst through the darkened embers, bringing it back to life. Fuelling the fire as high as he could, he filled a large pot with rainwater and set it above the flames to warm. It was seven in the morning, and Margaret was still sleeping. A large pot of hot tea sat on the table in the kitchen. By this time he had already cleaned the stable and fed the pig and the chickens the latter of which were now scuttling and squawking all around the yard, scratching for worms and insects.

Another quick mug of tea, he thought as he poured it, and he was off across the field to milk the goats. The clatter of wheels going over the stones in the lane brought him to his feet. It was Reagan, with Star pulling the yellow and blue Sunday cart, with Dandy tied up and travelling behind them.

"Tom!"

"Reagan," he called back. "Tea?"

"Why thank you, Tom," he replied, as Tom unhitched Dandy who was covered in white candle wax, grease and shoe polish, looking a total mess. Putting him straight into the paddock with Daisy, he did his regular thing, going straight for the dust pit, rolling and rolling with sheer delight before then racing and chasing Daisy all around the field in sheer excitement at being back at his farm.

Margaret put her head out of the cottage door, she was still half asleep. "Oh, Jesus, Mary and Joseph, and all the angels, thank you. Is he okay?" she asked, a smile breaking on her weary, craggy face.

"He's fine, Mam!" he replied to her.

"Breakfast?" she asked them both.

"Thank you, Margaret," Reagan replied, tipping his hat.

The goats now had to wait. Within 30 minutes of getting Dandy back out of the field, they had all the grease, shoe polish and candlewax from his body, and they dyed his hooves, and cut the feather hair from his fetlocks. They both stood in sheer admiration of their handiwork; he looked truly amazing, right back to his old self, a red chestnut roan, with a stand out flaxen mane and tail, a real beauty. Margaret nearly burst with pride on seeing Dandy back to his old self.

"Breakfast is ready," Margaret called out from the kitchen.

Tom and Reagan quickly tidied away all signs of their work, and put Dandy back into the field to graze alongside his mother. The visit came quicker than expected, the sound of tyres scrunching on the stones up the long lane making Margaret jump.

"Who could that be at this time in the morning?" she remarked.

"Everyone stay calm!" Tom instructed, as he wiped the bacon grease around the plate with his last piece of soda bread and popped it into his mouth.

"Who's in?" came the call from the gate.

Tom got to his feet telling Margaret and Reagan to stay seated with his raised hand. Margaret made the sign of the cross, kissed and fingered the crucifix on the rosary she now held in her hand as she sat waiting to see who was outside, and what they wanted, knowing instantly trouble was standing outside of her gate.

"Who's asking?" said Tom walking out into the yard.

A young red haired man stood in between two large thugs, a big white van parked in the lane behind them. "Shaun Flynn!" he called back.

"Well, Shaun Flynn what can I do for you, son?" Tom asked looking at this villainous trio.

"Who are you?" Flynn enquired spitting a large gob of spit right at Tom's feet, suddenly looking up and realising how big this man actually was. Even the two thugs looked nervously at one another.

"Tom Murphy," he replied, "and again I ask, how can I help you, son?"

"You're big Tom Murphy?"

"I am."

Flynn gulped. "I am looking for the black horse that beat my filly, he's a cover, a fake, running races, cheating good and fair folk!" he stammered at Tom.

"And why do you think he didn't win fair?" Tom asked him. "Beat you didn't he, so I hear."

"He was doped up, drugged, no horse like that could ever beat mine like that; it was a fix! That's what it was."

"Well, son why have you come to bother my mother?" Tom asked.

"Hear you beat Legacy some time ago, where's your racer?" Flynn asked, now slapping a very large shillelagh in his hand menacingly.

"Are you threatening me, son? Because if you are, you'll need more than the three of you," he told them firmly. "There he is in the field with his mother," he told Flynn, pointing at Dandy and Daisy stood together, nudging each other's necks. Dandy was doing the usual laid back thing, something he always did when he's happy and peaceful: his tongue was hanging out the side of his mouth; his ears were flopped out each side of his head, and his tail and mane glowing a glorious golden yellow in the morning sun.

"That thing is what beat Legacy?" Flynn asked in disgust. "I don't believe it, where is the black racer?" he asked nastily, with evil in his voice. The two thugs now huddled up behind him for support.

"Why ask me? What's it got to do with me? Neither me or either of those animals has ever raced against you, nor did my horse, which I hear has been killed, old gypsy revenge was it not?" he replied standing his ground.

Glancing again over in the field Flynn asked, "Why have you not raced him?"

"He's got a bad back, he'll never race again; I only did it because McConnell challenged me. Stupid bastard killed The General, fine horse that!" Tom replied still not moving and keeping direct eye contact with the aggressive young man in front of him, who was still slapping the large shillelagh in his hands.

"I'll be watching," Flynn told him in a spiteful manner.

"Will you now, lad, why?" Tom asked.

"Because I know you are hiding him somewhere, I have never in all my short years seen a horse with so fleet a foot, never with a turn so fast, it was almost as though he was bewitched, magical, the Devil's horse!"

"The Devil's horse?" Tom laughed out loud. "You don't know a lot about horses, lad, do you?" he quizzed.

"Enough to know when a fraudster is afoot, and foul play is in the air!" Flynn said walking menacingly towards Tom and swinging the large stick with intent.

Realising now that he would have to fight this stupid threesome, he let Shaun come at him, as he tried to figure out his next move. Tom ducked unexpectedly before landing a perfect smack on Flynn's nose. It exploded instantly sending shards of blood and cartilage over his face. Then Tom grabbed the other two thugs by their throats and bashed their heads together; the sickening crack of their skulls echoed around the yard. All three were now in a heap, so Tom picked up their sticks and threw them over the fence into the field next door.

Margaret and Reagan ran from the cottage to see what all the shouting had been about.

"Oh, dear Lord above, Tom what's happened?" Margaret asked anxiously.

"Well Shaun here and his two mates decided to pick a fight with me and lost."

"You fucker! I'll have you; my family will come and get you all!" Shaun screamed at Tom, getting to his feet and trying to stem the flow of blood. The two thugs had now struggled to their feet and stood holding their heads, wondering what the bloody hell had hit them.

Tom grabbed Flynn by the collar and held him up in the air, a good two feet off the ground, to face him. "Does Michael know that you are here," he asked him, "threatening me and my family?"

"How do you know my da?" Flynn asked shakily.

"Because we are related, we are cousins, and of course the one person we have in common is Uncle Billy."

"Oh shite, shite, sorry, Tom, please don't tell my da; please, he'll kill me."

"So well he should, you nasty little fucker. Do you honestly think I would shaft one of my own?"

"Oh no, no, never."

"Right, you and your mates fuck off, you hear me? Leave my family alone or I will be speaking with your family, and I will let Uncle Billy know what you have been up to, disrespecting our families here, got me?"

"Yes, sir," Shaun replied, sheepishly, blood still pouring from his flatted nasal opening as he turned to start to leave.

"Oh and, Shaun!" Tom called him. "You might think Uncle Billy is a bastard, but you haven't seen the other side of me. Ask him," Tom added as they were scrambling to get into the van to reverse down the long stony lane.

"Christ, Tom who is Uncle Billy?" asked Reagan.

"Someone you definitely don't ever want to meet," replied Margaret, relieved it was all over. "You okay, son?" she asked him.

"Fine, Mam. I will have a word with Michael though, nasty little shite, he needs sorting," he replied, making a mental note to speak to Michael when they next met.

It was a quiet night, and Reagan went home to a busy café, Claire busy serving apple pie, teas and rough cider. Little Tommy had lit the forge, and five donkeys and a pony stood patiently waiting for his attention. Reagan suddenly felt so guilty; he could have ruined everything and so easily have lost it all through his greed. He also acknowledged the pain and stress that he had caused Tom and Margaret. It could have all gone so wrong. He made a decision there and then that no matter what happened in the future he would never race the gypsies every again!

Tom was also taking note of his mother, sadly realising all was not well and that she really would not be able to stay in her lovely cottage for very much longer. It was all beginning to go downhill, and so was she. Margaret could hardly manage the veg patch, or to see to the animals without help anymore, and once again, and very painfully, the heartstrings pulled at him.

"Move the family here!" his mind told him.

"No," came Margaret's response, "you can't, love, it just won't work!" she told him.

Anxiety had now set in. Tom couldn't understand why his two sisters never bothered with his mother. Both were married to affluent men, yet they stayed away, it was as though they were embarrassed to acknowledge her.

I have to do something that will help her, he thought quietly to himself.

Chapter 23

Saving Dandy

SHAUN FLYNN WAS STILL SMARTING from his defeat at the fayre. Tom had indeed spoken to Michael, Shaun's father, who in a rage at his son's dishonourable actions had given him ten lashes with his belt for the trouble, after apologising to Tom for the bother and distress he had caused Tom's family. Tom graciously accepted his apology and they shook hands and left friends, which was all he really wanted.

Daisy pulled the cart from the meeting at the *Royal Oak;* she was enjoying the work, dancing and prancing, showing off her new shiny shoes, but Tom was still worrying. He knew that Shaun Flynn was an evil little toad and would want vengeance for his father's hiding. He also sensed that he'd come looking for Dandy again, watching the farm, paying for information, uncovering every stone possible in his search for the black racer.

At 19, Shaun was the youngest son of Michael and Molly Flynn. A large and strict Catholic family. They were landowners just on the outskirts of Dungarvan, some 20 miles away. Michael and Molly loved all of their children, but Shaun was an unexpected surprise and became the spoilt child, enjoying more than most children of his age, having his own pony and cart at the tender age of 6. It was at this time in his life that his passion for equine animals was discovered. He soon became known as the horse brat, his two older brothers having very quickly taught him how to fight, and his mother Molly spoiled him rotten. It was a bad combination and it made a nasty, tough, little beggar, who always seemed to get his own way. He very quickly formed a gang as soon as he went to school, and became known as a bully, and very soon, he was disliked by most families that knew him.

Racing became his passion, winning his first ever race at the age of 10. His father was so impressed that he started to buy and invest in racing stock to breed from, hoping one day to have bred his own all Ireland champion. Racing and wagering therefore became Shaun's life, and woe betides anyone who got in his way. His real passion, however, was winning and at any cost. He made sure that he always won, well as much as he could without cheating. He was shocked when he lost to Reagan. He had been around horses all his life, even working at the local racing stable, just to find out how they did things, and how he could use that knowledge in his racing.

He was a clever boy, had it all up top, and had been deep in the mix of it all, the racing stables, training, and attending races with his father, all to gain further knowledge which might give him an advantage. Yes, Shaun knew the good ones and the bad ones, and when he saw the turn of speed and sure footedness of the black racer, he instantly knew that was no ordinary farm horse, and he wanted it, dead or alive! Mind you, he hadn't counted on meeting up with big Tom Murphy. The hiding from his da was well deserved, he knew that, but the racer was being hidden from him he knew that. It was almost within touching distance, he could taste and smell him he was so close, but muddy waters ran deep, clouding his vision and senses. However, he knew that he was rarely wrong.

Margaret had noticed one or two odd people coming up and down the stony lane, which in turn was driving Daisy mad, as she thought they were having visitors, but they were not the kind they were used to. One day, Margaret saw a large man actually walking behind the cottage and go all around the back field. Now she didn't feel threatened, but it did start to worry her as they were in the middle of nowhere, without any close neighbours. Why were these men stalking around her house she wondered? Margaret told Reagan and he started to worry instantly, as Shaun Flynn came to mind. He decided to ring Tom that very night and told Margaret not to worry as he left her, but inside he was shaking. It was inevitable, Dandy would have to be found a new home, and fast. Shaun Flynn was still looking for trouble and still smarting from being beaten, and although he had been quiet for a while, he was sending spies to look for the black racer. Once again Reagan felt shame and disappointment that he had let everyone down and spoiled everything. He would remind himself every day for the rest of his life of his silly mistake.

Reagan called in on his dear friends Ellie and Brendan, who were at that moment admiring Dandy's offspring.

"We are never selling either of them," Ellie told him with pride, as she brushed the beautiful female hinny.

She had a lovely grey roan coat, and had the look of her father about her. They had called her Dancer. She was a beauty, and the little colt, which was now a big colt standing about 14 hands, was amazing, definitely Dandy's son. They had called him Comet, because he ran like one. Brendan and Ellie feared that one day the same thing would happen to either Comet or Dancer as had happened to their beloved Arthur and were constantly watchful.

Yes, they would keep them both for breeding, so pleased were they with their new offspring; these two would create a new bloodline for their stock, which in turn would keep the demand and price nice and high.

"Reagan come and have some tea, will you?"

"Why thank you, Ellie," he replied, never missing an offer of tea and cake with Ellie.

She, like Claire was a great cook. He watched them put the stunning duo back into the field and headed into their vast kitchen, breaking down into floods of tears as he sipped his tea, telling them both about the race, and how Shaun Flynn was trying to find Dandy and how his life was now in danger. It just came tumbling out from his lips like a babbling brook.

They instantly came to his side, comforting their dear and loved friend, reassuring him that no one was perfect, and the fact that we all made mistakes made us human. They told him they would help; it made Reagan feel so much better, being able to get it off of his chest, unloading this terrible burden he had walked around with, and the fact they hadn't judged him for his silly actions, just like Tom, made him realise he had true friends. Why was he so lucky, he asked himself? He thanked the Lord above and said a quiet prayer while he was nibbling the delicious fruit cake and then sipping his tea with bleary tear-filled eyes.

Brendan jumped up and put a hand on Reagan's shoulder, thinking out loud. "We just might be able to help," he told him.

Ellie was already on the phone and once her conversation had finished she asked Reagan, "Do you have Tom's telephone number?"

He nodded, fumbling in his jacket pocket for the tatty piece of paper with Audrey Collings' number on.

It was now midday, Saturday, and the phone rang in Audrey's home. The quick conversation made her heart race, gave her butterflies in her stomach, and a shuddering excitement rose in her.

"Hang on, Ellie, I'll go next door!" she told her, quickly changing her blouse for something sexier, applying lashings of deep red lipstick, and changing out of her slippers into high-heeled stilettos, before charging around to the Murphy house, and viciously banging on the bright yellow door.

Tom answered. "Audrey, what ails?" he asked.

“Ellie’s on the phone, trouble with Dandy!”

“Oh no,” he said, calling to Megan who was in the kitchen. “I’m going next door to the phone.”

“No worries, Dad,” she replied, sensing trouble and her father having to leave for Ireland again.

She wasn’t wrong. Tom returned and his face said everything. He packed after explaining the worrying situation and walked down the road one hour later, his holdall packed and his fists clenched ready to knock out, bloody Shaun Flynn. He headed once again for Temple Meads Station and the ferry to Rosslare, leaving Megan and Trixie in floods of tears, knowing how hurt their beloved grandmother, and of course Daisy would be at losing Dandy and having to send him away.

Reagan was waiting at the harbour in Rosslare when the ferry docked. The sea was rough, storm force seven, and it had been a bad crossing. The large white and green ferry banged into the harbour wall, and a loud crunching sound echoed around the dockside, as a large section of the bow crumpled under the impact. Screams of very frightened and seasick passengers could be heard above the howling wind.

“Oh heaven,” commented Reagan, as he watched the sailors and the ground deckhands struggle to tie her to the berth.

For 10 minutes he watched the dangerous and very frightening scenario play out in front of him, the ferry rising like a wild stallion on the end of a lasso as the massive waves smashed against her bows.

Eventually placated, the large ship started to behave, and they managed to tie her to the massive mooring bollards, and secure her against the dock. The relieved passengers tumbled down the gangplank signing themselves with the cross, when their feet hit terra firma; glad to be back in Ireland, and on solid ground, off the boat that had given them all a violent roller-coaster ride over the Irish Sea.

Both men were silent as Reagan drove them to Margaret’s house;

Shaun Flynn was now in serious trouble. Tom had managed to call his father Michael, straight after his call with Ellie, who of course had no idea what he had been up to again, explaining to Tom he had already taken the belt to him over the matter.

"Tom if he and his thugs show up again and frighten Margaret, I wash my hands of him, do what you will, that spoilt brat needs a lesson."

Tom had thanked him, and then pulled Audrey's arms away from his waist, which she was holding onto very tightly.

"Oh, lover come upstairs with me!" she pleaded, resisting his efforts to release his arms.

Christ she's bloody strong, he thought, eventually managing to release himself, Audrey falling into a crumpled heap on the floor.

"Tom!" she called out, putting out her arm towards him.

"Sorry, Audrey, emergencies in Ireland have to be dealt with," he said leaving as quickly as possible, relief flooding him; he'd managed once again to escape from the clutches of the neighbourly man eater.

Two men were standing at the gate looking into the yard at Margaret's cottage. Reagan had dropped Tom at the bottom of the long stony lane. It was a dank, overcast morning, and the two men were concentrating on looking over the gate. Tom was on foot, silent as he tiptoed up towards them, picking through the soft grassy patches growing in the lane. When he was close enough, he dropped his holdall and ran towards them catching them both by the neck at the same time, and dropping them onto the floor in one quick swoop. They fell like a pair of skittles, screaming in fear as their faces bashed into the soft mud at the bottom of the gate. Margaret heard the screams and rushed from inside the cottage to see Tom manhandling the two men who had been hanging about the farm that morning.

"Tom don't hurt them!" she called, fear pushing out of her aura and up into the ether asking for angelical help.

He picked the two squirming men up off the ground, and held them both very firmly against the gate. Their muddy faces and wild frightened eyes told the story.

"Now then, lads, what are you up to?" he asked them, his hands attached to each of their throats as he turned them around to face him.

Squirming, they kept silent, shaking their heads in defiance. "We can't say, sir, he'll kill us both," one of the young men replied.

"Who will, Shaun Flynn?" he asked. Their eyes widened even more. "Well?" Tom again asked increasing the pressure a little more.

"Okay, okay!" the other man said. "Yes, it's Shaun Flynn, wants us to watch out for the black racer, he knows you are hiding him somewhere, he wants revenge, he'll kill your stock if you don't give him up," he told him, now struggling for breath as he spoke.

"Tom!" called Margaret, who had been watching the whole thing from a distance, her face pleading with him not to throttle them both.

He released them. "Why do you think he's here?"

"Shaun knows he's here, somewhere, paid us both to watch every move. You are going to make a mistake at some point, and when you do he'll have you all," he told him with a venom that made Tom want to react and smash his face in.

"Is that so? What a fool! Can you see the racer here?" he asked both of them very calmly, shaking with rage and indignation, trying to keep from losing his cool and breaking both of their necks. "Well, lads you can give Mr Flynn a message: Tom Murphy is back and the racer is not here!" he spat at them with disgust written all over his face. He grabbed them both and turned and threw them back down the lane, kicking them up the behind as they stumbled onto the stones. They quickly composed themselves and ran down to the end of the lane, disappearing into the distance.

"Oh, son I have been so worried," Margaret instantly told him.

"Aye, Mam sorry! It's Flynn again, he's after Dandy. We need to talk," he told her gently as he went and retrieved his holdall, locking the gate behind him, and followed her into the cottage.

The whickering from the field gate brought him straight back out again, with two warm apples in his hands. Daisy was at the field gate, Dandy at her side, waiting for their expected treat, which they always received. Daisy was so excited that Master Tom was back, as it probably meant work pulling the cart, and she did her little dance on the spot with excitement.

"Later, girl!" he told her lovingly, scratching her under the chin, and looking at Dandy with his floppy ears, and kind face as he scrunched his juicy apple. A tear slowly crept from the corner of Tom's eye as he looked down at this gentle beast who had harmed no one, and had just ran and won a great race, and now because of Reagan's stupidity he was in mortal danger. The decision had been made, he said goodbye to the pair, and walked towards the cottage.

Both Daisy and Dandy stopped munching their juicy apple, bits falling onto the ground, huge donkey tears falling from their eyes. A new day was dawning, change was all around them, and Daisy somehow knew that Dandy would be leaving her. Dandy read her mind, and they cuddled together at the gate, big golden drops of tears plopping on to the dry dusty earth below.

Margaret's sobs and distress could be heard from the gate. Tom emerged wiping his eyes, and set about the chores, his core rocking, sad memories of his beloved greyhound, Prince, engulfing his mind. Why was it this place always pulled on his heart? He was strong, but always weak here on his emerald isle. Perhaps it was his love for this place, the people, and the animals that he carried with him in his mind? Here they nibbled at his heart. He felt sick to the stomach, wanting at that very moment to be anywhere else but there. He could sense the two girls back home in England crying; this was a painful moment for them all.

Daisy didn't dance when the Sunday cart was brought out of the barn. She was stood at the end of the field comforting Dandy, memories flooding her being, distress rising to the surface of her skin, reminding her of the day she and her friends were separated from their mothers. She remembered calling and calling for her, the pain inside was indescribable, and now her beautiful Dandy was leaving her she was sure.

Everything was unusually quiet, the Sunday cart stood by the gate, and she could still hear Mistress Margaret sobbing, so deep was her pain. Only the skylarks call echoed on the breeze flowing gently through the field; the atmosphere was sombre.

Tom walked into the field towards them. Daisy could see the pain that showed in his face, his red swollen eyes talked of the sorrow that walked beside him.

"Daisy girl, I'm sorry, Dandy is in danger, the gypsies want to kill him, we must send him away to a new home where he will be safe," he told her as he cuddled her furry head, his tears trickling down beside hers.

"It's okay, Master Tom, I always knew this day would come, at least I have the chance to say goodbye, something I never had!"

He turned to Dandy, who knew this was real love for him. "I'm sorry, son, you really are in serious danger, if the gypsies find you that would be a disaster you know that don't you, and you also know we all love you?" he told him, now cuddling them both together in his arms.

"It's okay, Master Tom," said Daisy, now realising that this was going to happen, and with that final moment of acceptance, they turned and walked slowly to the gate, Dandy going towards a new destiny.

Margaret was distraught on seeing Dandy tied to the back of the Sunday cart, and she fell to her knees, wailing into her skirts; her beloved Dandy was leaving. Daisy on seeing the distress of her mistress pulled the cart over to where she was on her knees and put her warm muzzle onto her forehead.

"Oh, Daisy lass!" she cried hugging her head. Daisy just stood over her and let her cry into her neck, just like before. This was her mistress, her mother had told her to be good for her new mistress, so she had to be strong for Margaret, masking her own tears and pain; it was her job. Margaret got up and went over to Dandy and kissed his muzzle, stroking his head. "Sorry, love, so sorry, but you have a lovely new home waiting for you, we love you and we will miss you always, please don't forget us."

"Never, Mistress," he told her.

Tom stopped what he was doing, turned and looked at Margaret. He had just heard Dandy's words of love to Margaret, they had brought back the tears, and he welled up again, pinching himself hard on the hand to try and distract himself from the heart breaking situation unfolding in the yard.

The pain was just too much to bear as he drove the cart out of the yard. Dandy was following, tied up at the back, and Tom could still hear his mother wailing as he left the stony lane and got onto the road that led to Gory. They were headed for Ellie and Brendan's farm. He pushed Daisy on; they needed to get to their farm as quickly as possible, but first just a little detour to his friend Gerald Malone, the knacker man.

Tom pulled up outside the knacker yard, far away enough for his steeds not to smell the odour of blood that wafted away on the breeze. He didn't want Dandy to think that he was ending up here.

"Gerald!" he called as he entered the yard.

"Who's asking?" came the reply.

"Tom Murphy!" he called back.

Gerald instantly came out of a stone barn, blood dripping from his long apron, a massive knife in his hand, and long leather gloves up his arms.

"How the devil are you, Tom?" he asked.

"In a pickle, Gerald, can you help me?" he asked him with honesty in his voice.

"What is it, Tom?" he asked again.

"Flynn wants my horse, the one that beat Legacy; he's out to kill it. I heard you shot one similar looking today. Could I tell him it's mine?" he asked gulping.

"Oh, Tom I'm so sorry for your trouble. Yes I have been hearing, nasty little bastard that one. Margaret upset?"

"Mortified," said Tom, lowering his head.

"He's still in the lorry; I'm so busy I haven't had time to butcher him yet. Come take a look," Gerald invited him, as they walked towards the lorry where the crumpled remains lay. He lowered the back ramp, and a sharp bullet hole straight between the eyes stood out. "Didn't suffer!" he said with pride.

"I know," replied Tom, amazed; the markings and the size really could be Dandy's double. Tom reached into his pocket and took out a twenty pound note, handing it to Gerald.

"What's that for?" he asked almost in disgust. "Put it away, it's about time that nasty little fucker had his comeuppance. Tell Flynn Dandy broke his front right running around the field and I shot him at your place, which is why Margaret is so heartbroken.

Okay?"

"Thank you, friend," Tom said, putting his hand out and shaking Gerald's.

"So sorry for your trouble, Tom, but don't worry we'll sort him," he said closing up the ramp and saying a quick goodbye before going back into his barn to finish butchering his carcass.

Tom made for Ellie and Brendan's once again, pushing Daisy on, arriving just as the afternoon sun started to lose its heat. Daisy suddenly freaked, whickering in distress, seeing the very lorry that had taken her to the sale. It sat in the yard in its usual place.

"Steady, girl!" he reassured her as she brought the cart into the yard. She knew this place, remembering her mother and her birth, and panic quickly took her. "Daisy!" Tom again called her. She relaxed, but only just.

Brendan and Ellie came straight out of the kitchen to greet them both, Reagan following behind them, very sheepishly; you could see that he had been crying. Brendan shook Tom's hand, but Ellie just rushed over to Dandy.

What an animal, she thought, stroking him and wishing he was there at their stud to service their mare and keep producing amazing offspring for them. But alas, it was not to be, Dandy was heading for England where a friend of theirs owned a lovely stable that worked with riding for the disabled. Recently a horse had died leaving them short. All the animals they owned were donated, and when Ellie made the call, they were praying for another animal, instantly accepting Dandy, thanking the Lord above for their luck, sending a horse lorry immediately to Fishguard to meet the morning ferry from Rosslare. They wanted this horse, and wanted him bad, especially as the Olympic Committee had just accepted disabled riders into the games, and they had been given funding for riders – all they needed was the horses, and guess what? They had just found one.

Tom signed the papers that would accompany Dandy through the veterinary screening at the port in Rosslare and then over to England; official veterinary papers that Ellie and Brendan always used to sell and transport their stock out of Ireland. Well known to the board, Dandy would be passed without any hesitation, no questions asked; it would be a quick rubber stamp job, so well-known were they for their honesty and integrity.

Brendan started up the lorry and Daisy let out a cry, whickering to Dandy.

"It's okay, Mum, I'll always think of you and love you," he told her.

Ellie suddenly remembered Daisy being parted from her mother and instantly went over to her. "It's okay, Daisy, he's going to be fine, he's going to a wonderful home where loads of disabled children will ride and compete on him in the Olympics. How wonderful is that, your son competing with disabled children on top, how proud must you be of your son?" she whispered in her ear, while stroking her ears, seeing the donkey tears fall as Dandy muzzled her goodbye, and was loaded onto the back of the lorry, but not before Tom approached him giving him a loving hug.

"Thank you for everything, the race I mean."

"No need to thank me, Master Tom, your father Miles told me we would race, he always wanted you to, he was sad he died so suddenly, he had big plans for you."

"Thank you," Tom said, gently kissing him on the head. "Dandy!"

"Yes, Master?" he replied, looking at Tom.

"I see gold medals around you, son."

"I know," Dandy replied.

"Yes, yes you do!" His hand rubbed along his back as he passed, gently going up the ramp into the lorry.

Daisy whickered, "Goodbye, son!"

"Bye, Mother!" came the call back as the chunking noise of the ramp closed, the engine revved and the lorry pulled away; that was the last she would ever see of him again.

Tom held her close as they watched him leave, going away to a new life. All Tom had to deal with now was Shaun Flynn, and after today he had better be ready to face him, because Tom was now ready for a fight with Shaun Flynn, one Shaun would most definitely lose.

The ride home was quiet, Daisy not her usual self, Tom reflecting again on what had just happened, worrying about having to face his distraught mother when they got back to the cottage. They pulled into the yard and Daisy was sombre. Margaret came straight out of the cottage to Daisy, hugging and blessing her. Dandy's presence was missed already and there would not be a dry eye in the household tonight.

***

SHAUN FLYNN MADE HIS WAY up the stony lane in the white van accompanied by his usual two thugs. Daisy heard them coming first, whickering to Tom who was in the stable. He was decluttering and rearranging it inside, making it more comfortable for Daisy.

"Tom Murphy!" came the call from Shaun Flynn who was stood at the gate.

"Why, it's Shaun Flynn, what can I do for you, son?"

"I know you lost your racer, sorry!"

"Now how do you know that?" he asked him.

"Gerald Malone told da and I went to see him, saw the racer in the lorry, sorry, Mr Murphy!"

"Yes, a freak accident, Margaret's distraught," he told him.

"Yes it hurts losing a good horse," he said tipping his hat and getting back into the van to return home.

"Lord please thank Gerald Malone," Tom said signing himself with the cross, and going into the cottage to tell Margaret what had just happened.

Chapter 24

A sad time

TIME WAS NOT KIND TO Margaret, within weeks of losing her beloved Dandy, she suffered a stroke, and once again, much to the frustration of the family, Tom journeyed to Ireland. Margaret was being looked after in St Joseph's hospital in Enniscorthy, being cared for by the Catholic nursing sisters. She was very weak, and her mind and speech were sluggish, but she was recovering.

Tom arrived back at the cottage, Reagan once again having been kind enough to pick him up from the ferry. The cottage was dirty, unkempt, cold and unwelcoming. Daisy on the other hand was fine, in good fettle, although she was fretting and worried about where on earth her mistress was.

It was Reagan that found Margaret on the floor that painful day, driving like a madman down to Gory to use the telephone and call an ambulance. As soon as Margaret was taken to St Joseph's hospital, Monsignor Doyle was notified. Reagan had been calling every day to make sure Daisy was fed and watered, feeling her worry and loneliness on the little farm in the middle of nowhere, with not a neighbour in sight. In all honesty anything could have happened to her. Tom suddenly realised the situation was futile, but in a funny way though, it was a blessing that Dandy had found a lovely new home, it would be one less thing to worry about.

That night Daisy stood at the stable door, the half top of which was open, watching Tom while he cleaned and started to prepare his evening meal.

"Oh, Mam what a bloody mess!" he said softly to himself, stroking Daisy's nose as she was trying to open the bolt on the door. This was one of her old tricks, which Margaret always chastised her for, but even though she didn't tell her, Margaret loved the little tricks she got up to, always making her so proud of how clever she was.

Once the house was clean and sparkling and his supper bubbling away in the large black pot hanging over the fire, he went outside, made a fire in the fire pit, lit the two oil lamps on either side of the front door and sat down in front of the fire pit. With a hot mug of tea in his hands, and Daisy beside him, they both quietly stared into the flames and wondered what on earth happened next.

"Don't worry, Master Tom you will sort it all out."

"Well thank you, lass, I need you to be strong for Mam now!" he told her quietly.

"Oh, Master Tom, I will," Daisy replied honestly, "she's my mistress and I love her."

"I know you do, Daisy, and I have never had the chance to tell you we all love you, and thank you so much for being in ours and Mam's life."

Daisy stood for a second, a little shock running through her; life now meant something, she was loved and needed, and now she knew it for sure, it made her happy, and big, sloppy donkey tears slid down her muzzle. At last, for the first time in her life, she knew her purpose and what she was meant to be - Margaret's companion, bound in this world and in mind; they would always be together, forever. Of that she was sure.

DAISY WHICKERED LOUD AS SHE heard the tyres scrunching on the stones in the lane, a signal of someone arriving. It was early morning, Tom was milking the goats in the top field, and her whickering caught his attention. He thanked the goats for the precious milk he had collected and made his way down the field. His two sisters, Annie and Tricia stood in their fine expensive clothes outside the cottage door, their rich husbands Donal and Andrew wandering around the yard sizing everything up, making notes and commenting on the amount of land the cottage stood in.

"Annie! Tricia! What a sight for sore eyes! What in heaven can I do for you today?" he asked them.

"We have come to talk about Mam," they both said in unison.

"Really? I am shocked, in all the years you have both been married, neither of you have ever bothered with mother, even when she was nearly starving! Strange that! I have been coming over here every 6 weeks or so when I am needed, but she's not even seen a hair on your heads for years. Why now?" he asked, confused, and very worried. What was this, he questioned himself?

The two husbands pretended not to hear the conversation, and carried on chatting, nodding heads, looking out into the paddock as their wives spoke with Tom, just listening in case of any raised voices.

"Well, you'd better come in. Tea anyone?" he asked filling the large black kettle hanging over the fire, which was spitting out sparks. The pine kindling sticks were full of resin and the scent wafted up the chimney and around the little room, smelling of trees and forests which were just behind the house. "Please sit down, ladies," he bade them, but they were already turning their noses up at the shabbiness of the little cottage, not really wanting to sit on the worn settle or chairs. "What's the matter, girls, not good enough for you? Shame – remember, you were both born and lived here, it's your old home." Both his sisters looked at him with humiliation written all over their faces, immediately bowing their heads; it was as though they were actually afraid to sit down. “Right then, what do you want?” He never minced his words with them. “All these years and neither of you have ever bothered with your own mother, and now you are here with your posh and very rich husbands, so what do you want?” he again asked quite forcefully.

“Mam’s not going to be able to stay here is she? What’s going to happen to the farm?” Annie asked, turning a full blown shade of red as the words spluttered from her mouth.

Tom stopped for a second, and looked at his two sisters, greed showing in their faces. They had good husbands, with very large bank balances, and they wanted for, or needed nothing. They had never bothered with their mother, even when at times she was near starvation, and here they were now, having the front to ask what was going to happen to the farm when she moves – money - it always came down to money with them.

Tom suddenly felt ashamed, it was like a bolt coming out of the blue, he had bought his mother’s farm, not even thinking about his own family back in England, who were also very hard up, and had not a slice of luxury for themselves. He thought of his beautiful Patsy, who slaved away when she could making do with second-hand everything. He had exchanged his winnings for the farm, when in fact he could have bought his own home and given his family a better life, but he was thinking about the promise that he had made to his father that if anything should ever happen to him, which sadly it did, dying suddenly and leaving the family to fend for themselves, that he would look after his mother. Tom had kept that promise, but at a loss to him and his beautiful family, and now seeing the vultures had started to circle, he realised that he had totally let his own family down. How could he have been so blind and so very stupid?

***

LOGAN ABRAHAM WAS THE LOCAL lawyer and his advice struck Tom like a serrated knife through the heart. Margaret's next of kin which was him, Annie and Tricia would be entitled to inherit an equal share of the farm on Margaret's death, even though he had purchased the house for her. It was a gift, and the farmhouse and land had all been passed to her, all done legally by the council solicitor, and there was nothing Tom could do about it. Margaret's health and state of mind would not allow a power of attorney or even a new will to be made. The words hit hard, words that Tom would never forget: "Shame you didn't get any advice, Tom, you should have come to me," he told him as he shook his hand, shaking his head at the very sad situation around them both.

Keiron and Mary O'Donnell lived on the outskirts of Gory not far from the little tiny town of Arklow. At 45, Keiron had retired from the armed Garda, a bad fall one day chasing a suspected IRA terrorist having put paid to his work in the force, and a fractured spine had left him partially paralysed and in a wheelchair. He would think about that day for the rest of his now miserable life. He was Miles' (Tom's father) nephew, and had married a lovely girl called Mary, only 6 months before the accident. Any hopes of a family were totally dashed, and their lives had become a miserable slog, Mary blaming Keiron, and he in turn blaming those bastard IRA men for the void left in their lives. Never would they know the joy of a child in their arms, and it was at times as if they even resented being alive, so bad was the hurt inside.

Soon though, lady luck smiled on them, and life became more bearable. When Keiron's father passed away suddenly one night in his sleep, they inherited his father's lovely house. It was very smart, and painted red green and white, set in three acres of land, with an annex attached to the side of it, and a lovely stable and barn at the back. It was indeed a notable place and they had made a point of saying hello to Margaret and Tom at the wedding, letting everyone know about their good fortune, and everyone had wished them well. Bad luck had been around them now for some time, and it was pleasing news that they were re-joining the land of the living with purpose.

Tom never really knew why he didn't take to either of them, and was surprised one day when they approached him, offering the annex for Margaret to live in, plus the stable and field for Daisy. At the time it seemed like the answer to Tom's prayers, but, little did Tom know that Annie and Tricia had been hatching a plot to get Margaret out of the farm, so they could sell it, and take their share, offering a nice little reward to Keiron and Mary. It was a plan that was now coming together nicely as Margaret had been taken ill.

Tom visited Keiron and Mary in their lovely house; they seemed nice enough, very concerned about Margaret and Daisy, and at least in the annex she would be close to them. She would be safe and looked after, they told him, and reassuring words of kindness and support lulled him into a false sense of security and he agreed with them. He didn't really have much choice; he was stuck with nowhere to go. Margaret could never return to the farm on her own, the nursing sisters at the hospital had insisted firmly, and although the old heartstrings pulled, he knew they were right. There with Keiron and Mary, she would have her own lovely room, running water, plumbed in bath and toilet, and Daisy right next door. Taking her home to England with him was also not an option, although he had actually thought about it. Patsy was still very ill, he was only just coping with her going in and coming back out of hospital all the time, and coping with his four children. No, he couldn't see any other option, or way to deal with this difficult situation, so begrudgingly, he accepted Keiron and Mary's offer.

Margaret and Daisy moved in one week later. Tom had cut the front door in half, just like the one on the farm, which meant that Daisy could stand at the door and poke her head in keeping an eye on his mother. Her bed was right next to the door, and a cosy sofa and small table framed the corner of the room. She had a little sink with running water, and a lovely stove to cook on. The small hearth was just right for a little warming fire, a bathroom out the back, and a little scullery, with a larder where she could do her washing and prepare and store her food.

Tom worked hard that week on the small annex, getting it ready, bringing all Margaret's belongings, and making it feel like a real home for her. Daisy was ecstatic, as she was getting to pull the cart two or three times a day. Tom used the work cart, it was flat and he could move all her bits and pieces easily, tying it all down securely for the journey ahead.

He sent the pig to slaughter, but the chickens and goats he gave to Ellie and Brendan; it was the least he could do after their help with Dandy, and Daisy finally moved in the very day that Margaret came home from hospital. Her stable was dry and very warm, and he installed a large water trough, and made a large fire pit outside, and filled the barn with all the hay and straw from his farm, which would see her through the rest of the year easily.

When it was all done he took a last look around the farm. Daisy was pulling the Sunday cart now, as he'd sold the work cart to one of Ellie and Brendan's neighbours. There was absolutely nothing left, only the wheat bending in the warm winds, and the empty house, barn and pig sty, waiting for their new, loving owners. This would be the last time he would ever see the cottage again, and his whole life suddenly flashed before him. Turning and saying goodbye to it all as Daisy pulled him out of the gate for the last time, a single tear fell from both of their eyes as they made their way down the stony lane, and past the large sign which said 'For auction' as they made their way to the new house.

It all went well at the beginning, Margaret's farm sold for a massive twelve hundred pounds, three times what Tom had paid the council for it. Tricia and Annie very quickly instructed a solicitor to claim their inheritance, giving the cash to their greedy husbands who would use it for a new business they had been contracted to build and sell new homes for the local authority and their tenants. Yes, the plan had worked well, and now it was Keiron and Mary's turn to pull Tom's heartstrings.

Mary was attending Margaret every day, cooking and cleaning and generally keeping an eye on her. Daisy stood every day at the half opened door poking her head in, talking to her mistress and just being around her. Mary though didn't like animals, dirty smelly things, she always thought. Keiron refused to believe that she was a farmer's daughter, refusing to even have a cat or a dog for company, much to his annoyance, and Daisy totally irritated her. She just could not understand why Margaret wanted the dam animal around her all the time, getting into awkward confrontations when trying to push Daisy back into the field, much to Margaret's growing annoyance.

Daisy soon became a novelty, and word soon spread that Margaret Murphy and her hinny that drew a race with the famous General, had moved into Keiron and Mary O'Donnell's annex, and the funny sight of Daisy's rear end became a local talking point, even getting into the local paper, and on the local radio station. People would whistle or beep their horns as they passed, making Daisy excited, and Margaret chuckle. Every time this happened Daisy would do her little dance on the spot, and locals and other people around on hearing the funny news, would now actively go out of their way to pass her at Keiron's and Mary's place, just to see Daisy hanging over the door, and watch her little dance as she reacted to the much loved attention.

Mary was now absolutely infuriated, and she started giving Daisy the odd nasty slap on the rump when she passed her on her way to attend Margaret, moaning and grumbling about the smelly animal which blocked her way into the cottage, and was always messing outside the door. Mary really had no affection or interest for this animal, and only put up with this silly charade because of the money.

So for a while, Tom relied totally on Keiron and Mary to look after his mother and Daisy, giving them via Logan Abraham the local lawyer, the remaining money left over from the sale of the farm, which was three hundred and eighty pounds. It was a fortune at that time, and it was given in return for Keiron and Mary looking after Margaret and Daisy, to fund all their needs, and if his mother should die, to keep Daisy well and retired until her death. The money he passed over would more than exceed their needs, he knew that, but he was constantly questioning himself whether he had done the right thing. He was still struggling with his family back in England, his horrible greedy sisters had taken the money and run, and again disappeared out of Margaret's life, never visiting or even enquiring as to how she was, and with no other family help, again the whole caring package came down to Keiron and Mary. He felt relieved that he had actually paid them for the work, as this made him feel slightly better, albeit not much. Still though he did not know why he was felt so uneasy about the whole situation.

Six months later, Margaret suddenly died, succumbing to another stroke, she went peacefully in her sleep. She was laid to rest next to her beloved husband Miles. Hundreds of people turned out in respect for the Murphy family, Annie and Tricia sheepishly standing at the back of the church with their husbands. Tom stood alone in the front pew, Reagan, Ellie and Brendan, the pew behind, just being there to support Tom. He had chosen not to bring any of the family over for the funeral. Patsy could flare up at any time, and the two girls would be so upset at having to leave Daisy, already pleading with him to bring her home and put her on the allotment, so they could look after her, but that was just not possible, and the day he left for the funeral, walking down the road towards the bus stop, he could hear the howling and grief, he was leaving behind.

Daisy pulled the Sunday cart to the funeral. Tom had told her Margaret was gone, that it was her time, and that the angel beings had come and taken her to be with Miles her husband, and now Daisy knew she was all alone. After the funeral Tom made arrangements to make sure Daisy would be safe and well-looked after. Reagan would call every week to check on things, and Keiron and Mary would see to Daisy's daily needs. Audrey Collings' telephone number was written in their phone book. At this particular time, it really was the best he could do, reassuring Daisy she would be fine, but somehow she knew trouble was looming, and she was right in the middle of it.

Banned from the yard now, Daisy would stand by the field gate, gazing out onto the road, and the lovely apple tree at the end of the drive. Alone and lonely with no one's attention, Mary and Keiron hardly bothering with her at all, and not taking the proper care of her that they had promised, she felt lost, pining for Mistress Margaret, and often wondering where her beloved Dandy was now.

Her life had changed dramatically, but she was always pleased to see Reagan when he called to see her, but Keiron and Mary didn't like Reagan calling around.

"Nosy bastard!" they would always say, and there were always heated conversations and bad feelings when he left.

"Oh, Mistress I really miss you so much." Daisy would cry big donkey tears every time Reagan departed, not knowing if she would ever see him or Master Tom ever again.

Chapter 25

Daisy's decline

IT HAD BEEN 3 LONG lonely years for Daisy; standing at the gate, looking for someone; in fact anyone who was passing, to talk to her, or give her some affection that she so badly missed. Since Mistress Margaret had died, no one really seemed to take interest in this lonely, gentle beast, who had given her life working for a family and the one woman she loved more than anything, and here she was now, in a sparse muddy field, with hardly anything to eat and often without water enduring a miserable and very lonely existence. She now lived with Tom Murphy's relatives Keiron and Mary O'Donnell on the edge of Gory. Daisy was given a large 2 acre field with a lovely stable just across the yard, next to the little annex, which adjoined a large 4 bedroom brightly painted, red, white and green farmhouse which stood out a mile up and down the long road which led directly to Gory. It was surrounded by very tall hedges of trees, which looked glorious in the summer, and when empty of their leaves looked and sounded spooky in the dark and gloomy winter months, only to burst back to life again in the spring, once again bringing abundance and colour to an otherwise gloomy, unloved and lonely smallholding. This sadly was where Margaret spent the last months of her life. After she left hospital Tom had made an agreement with Mary and Keiron that they were to keep his inheritance on the understanding that when his mother passed, they would look after Daisy in her old years, and keep her right.

Although at the outset while Margaret was alive they had done just that, after she passed it all quickly changed and they spent most of their time in the local pub, or on holiday, never even bothering to look into the small paddock to see if Daisy was all right, or even alive. They just didn't care about the smelly, useless old hinny that their cousin worried about so much, sometimes smacking her when she called out to them as they came home full of liquor, pleading with them to fill her water butt so she could drink; it became a battle of the wills, and one that Daisy it seemed was losing. Even Reagan had stopped calling by, often scolded out of the gate by a drunken Keiron, with Mary cackling with laughter as she looked on, screeching at him at the top of her voice, that he was a softie, a donkey lover and not a real man, which of course, hurt and upset Reagan. After all, it wasn't his donkey; he was only calling over to make sure she was being looked after okay, just as he had promised his old friend Tom, but he had a wife and child now, and with his business being so busy, it was often a struggle just to get enough time to pop over. When this was coupled with the constant barrage of verbal abuse and threats he received from Keiron and Mary, the visits got less and less, and Daisy started to go downhill.

It was on his last visit, when Keiron and Mary were totally drunk, and threatened him with a large stick to get off their property, that Reagan decided enough was enough. He could see Daisy was not looking good, and was lame, and once again her water butt was empty. He decided to write to Tom in England, and tell him what was going on, and how worried he was about Daisy, and could he come, as the old girl might not have long? He felt great shame as he posted the letter, as he had always promised his friend to do his best, but felt at this moment in his life, he had let him down.

"Please, God, get Tom Murphy over here fast to deal with those two bastards!" he said inwardly as the letter slipped from his fingers into the deep darkness of the green box.

Daisy knew her life was coming to a close, so she waited and waited at the gate for Master Tom. She knew in her heart he would come soon, it had seemed years since she had last seen him, and angels were constantly around her, just like they were when young Megan came to stay, and when Margaret became ill. It was always a sign, Daisy knew. She felt ill all the time, she was constantly starving; there was nothing to eat that could nourish her in the sparse muddy hole of a field and she had taken to eating the thorny gorse which grew around the edge of her field, but little did she know, the flowers were a poison to her, and nasty sores and blisters were now appearing all around her mouth, and her tongue was swelling, at times making it almost impossible to eat. Her weeping eyes were full of puss that dribbled constantly down her face, and her badly matted dull coat was a sure telltale sign that she was in a bad way and in the last throes of her now miserable life.

She would often daydream, remembering her night of passion with Legend, giving life to Dandy her beautiful foal, often wondering where he was now, and of course, remembering her beautiful Mistress Margaret, and pulling the Sunday cart for her with pride. Oh, and she would never forget the race with the gypsies, making Master Tom beam with pride at the dead heat of her race. But it seemed that no one wanted the old working donkeys anymore in the new emerging Emerald Isle. The motor car had seen to that. New fandangled lorries, farm machinery, vans and tractors had replaced them, and most of them, just like Daisy, were left to rot, sometimes to just drop down dead in the field, left untouched until all that remained to see, was their bare bones, in a lonely field, often picked clean by the foxes, unloved, untouched and unnoticed by all. But the angels would look after her, she knew. They had told her so.

It was a very cold and wet winter, and sometimes Daisy was left out for days in the driving rain, as she could gain no access to her lovely stable, which was across the yard, next to the house. She could see and feel the warmth the stable would give her, so she called out as loud as she could to Keiron and Mary, who were always snug, mostly drunk in the house opposite, but to no avail, no one ever came. She would try and find shelter from the blistering sharp cold winds which would blow ragingly around the field, especially when they came from the north, attacking her; it always felt like little needles spiking her sore skin. She would stand with her head deep in the gorse for protection, with her rear poking out to the wind; it was the only way she could shield herself from the winter storms, but little did she know, she was only making matters worse, and the more she put her head into the gorse, the more poison was entering her now battered body.

The now old, beaten and rusty red Volkswagen beetle stood waiting outside Gory Station. Within minutes of arriving, the massive frame of Tom Murphy emerged on his own through the station door.

"Hi, Johnny," he called out as his cousin beeped the horn acknowledging him, getting out and hugging him in friendship.

"How the devil are ye and the family, Tom?" he asked him as he took his holdall from his large plate-sized hands, and strong muscular arms, and placed it with a huge puff and struggle on the back seat.

"Well, thank you, and the family here?" Tom asked excitedly, nodding and commenting as all the news spilled from his cousin's mouth. "How's Daisy?" he asked firmly, the question hit hard, making him suddenly quite nervous.

"Don't really know, Tom to be honest, Mary and Keiron look after her as you know, but they don't like anyone calling anymore, even Reagan is really upset not being able to go and see her, but the last time I saw her she didn't look too good," he replied feeling very ashamed.

"Has anyone called the vet out?" Tom again questioned, concern and worry for Daisy filling his head, making him feel quite sick with remorse he had left it so long to come back and check on her. With everything going on at home, it wasn't as if he didn't have enough to worry about. He'd left Patsy still poorly with only his four children to look after her.

"Are ye staying with Keiron and Mary, Tom?" Johnny asked, tentatively, trying to lighten the mood as he carefully drove through the misty rain which was darkening the grey and silver wintery skies.

"Yes I am, Johnny," he replied, biting his lip as rage had started to emerge through his skin.

"Well you can sort Daisy out then, Tom," Johnny replied, now himself feeling extremely sick thinking about the confrontation that Tom would be having with Keiron and Mary. God only knew why those two greedy pigs had taken all the money for themselves when Tom had sold Margaret's cottage. The money was intended for her nursing care and funeral, and what was left over would be used to look after Daisy, which he knew was exactly what Tom had agreed with them. That's why he had given them his share, but Margaret had died quicker than they thought she would, finally succumbing to a stroke, and Keiron and Mary had taken all the remainder of the money for themselves. This had caused an uproar in the family that was left to watch the greedy duo fall out of the pub 7 days a week, not attending to their small holding or Daisy, and all Tom wanted was for his mother's beautiful companion to be cared for in her last days, retiring from years of hard work, she deserved nothing more. But Johnny knew that Keiron and Mary had turned into a pair of drunkards, and had not been looking after Daisy at all, spending all the inheritance on themselves; he also knew that trouble was coming, and oh to be a fly on the wall of that house tonight. He'd drop Tom off at their house and leave immediately, he suddenly decided.

Beep, beep, beep! Johnny sounded the horn as they pulled in through the house gate. It was late afternoon, the clouds in the sky were a multicoloured web of silvers, greys and streaks of black coming in from the east and the wind was bitterly cold. Shards of rain which hurt as they hit the skin came down like little arrows, suddenly freezing your skin, bringing red welts to the surface just to remind you it was actually raining. The tall trees surrounding the large house added to the whole wintery scene making it foreboding and quite spooky. Darkness was slowly creeping her way in surrounding them all.

Tom released a sigh of relief, feeling in his pocket for the warm juicy apple he always brought for Daisy. Keiron and Mary suddenly appeared at the door, both looking terribly nervous, eyes shifting away from Tom as if trying not to look at him.

"See you tomorrow, Tom!" Johnny shouted very nervously as he struggled to unload the large holdall before quickly reversing the car and driving out of the gate as fast as he possibly could.

"Be Jesus, Tom, it's lovely to see you!" called Keiron, holding out his hand in a nervous welcoming manner, and at the same time bending down to pick up Tom's holdall.

Mary was standing quietly at the door looking very sheepish. "Tom how are ye and the family?" she asked him quietly.

"Well, thank you both. Is Daisy in her stable?" he asked in a strong quizzing tone.

"Oh we don't know," Keiron replied, shakily, fear creeping into his voice, as he threw Mary a very quick glare. It was as if he was asking her if she had put her into the stable, knowing damned well that they had not. Neither of them had actually looked at the poor old thing for the last week, not bothering to feed her or give her any water.

"Well?" Tom asked again. He already knew the answer of course, but rage was not ready to burst out of him quite yet. These two greedy bastards had always irked him, and he had been so sad when Margaret had agreed to come and live with them, because there was no other option available.

"Tom come in, we'll see to Daisy later. I've food on the table," she replied.

"Fuck your food, Mary, Daisy is more important. Where is she?" he asked now in a very firm and quite menacing manner.

"We don't know, Tom, somewhere out in the bottom field," Keiron frankly replied, now feeling terrible, admitting that they had not a care in the world about her.

Mary started screaming, she was panicking suddenly realising they were both in serious trouble. They had already been warned by Reagan just a month ago to feed her and give her water and put her into the stable, out of the sleety rain which was making her sick. He had told them both that she was now old and very frail when he called by, but when a very drunken Keiron threatened him with a large shillelagh to get off his land and mind his own business, Reagan had left and very quickly at that. Both had fallen into bed very drunk that night and had laughed themselves to sleep, but neither of them was laughing now, neither wanting to be on the end of Tom Murphy's wrath.

They had ignored Reagan's warnings and as a consequence an angry looking Tom Murphy now stood outside the house looking directly at them, wanting at that very moment in time, to break both of their scrawny drunken necks, but he had to see to Daisy first. He had to find her that was his priority not the bloody food on the table which he knew they thought would placate him. How wrong could they be?

Mary screeched a howl that could be heard half a mile away, and ran into the house. Keiron looked at Tom and gulped, and took a huge deep breath as he looked into the wild Irish eyes of the mountain of a man that stood towering above him. His face read of anger and sheer disgust.

"Tom please, it's just a fecking smelly old donkey." He trembled as he spoke.

"Well I'll have you and that bitch of a greedy wife of yours know that smelly old donkey was my mother's best friend, and when the cottage was sold, the money you received from me was paid to you with the written agreement of a solicitor that the money was not only to look after Mam, and bury her when the time came, but to also look after Daisy as well, because she was the best thing in my mother's life. She became her companion, and she loved her, and in return Daisy looked after Mam, and worked her heart out for her. All I wanted was for her to have a lovely retirement in her old age, and all you had to do, while you sat in your fancy red, white and green pile of shite, paid for with Mam's money, was to feed and water her, clean her stable and the field, and occasionally get Reagan in to see to her feet, not an awful lot to ask for while you sit in luxury was it?" he remarked.

"No, no, no, Tom, we're very sorry."

"Really? What for, Keiron?" Tom was now really angry and his blood was boiling. "What are you sorry for?" he again asked him as he placed his hand around Keiron's throat. "What are you sorry for, Keiron? I won't ask you again?"

"Oh God in heaven, please don't hurt me, I'm not well."

"Well you'll be even more unwell in a moment if you don't tell me," Tom told him, as he now heard Mary screaming from the doorway.

"Don't hurt him, Tom, I'll get the Garda."

"Yes, good, go on, get them, Mary," he replied, as he released Keiron's neck from his hand and turned shouting to them both, "if I find you have been in any way neglectful and harmed Daisy in any way, you'd both better pack your bags, and fuck off while I'm here, because I will not be responsible for my actions towards you both, understand?" He looked at Keiron and took a deep breath, tears filling his eyes and starting to roll down his cheeks in sheer anger and anguish at what he was going to find. Keiron and Mary scurried back into their home to quickly pack, leaving Tom standing outside the house, just trying in his head to work out what he was going to do first.

He set out to the stable; it was quite disgusting and stank, and couldn't have been cleaned out for years. Donkey manure was stacked up the wall in huge piles.

"Oh God, Daisy, I am so sorry," he cried to himself quietly as he set about clearing out all the filthy straw and dung into a large pile outside the stable to one side. He then filled the empty water trough with fresh sparkling rainwater from the large tank outside, and then he laid a large thick bed of straw which he found at the back in the shed which joined the little stable. He could see that it had been there for months totally untouched. Next he needed hay. The rain was still sending cold spikey needles which pricked his face and hands, as he worked going to and fro, making the stable fresh warm and clean again. When he walked to the back of the shed, behind the straw he found the hay, bales and bales of it, again, untouched. "Bastards," he muttered as he frantically worked. He soon had the stable ready. He was trying in his head not to believe that he would find her dead in the field like so many other poor animals that had died alone that year. He was praying out loud for help and protection from the angelical beings he knew were always with him and Daisy. He lit three large oil lamps which he had quickly filled, and hung them inside the now cosy stable. Darkness had crept in like a grey sleepy river as he worked, and he would now need some light outside. He found another two oil lamps, which he filled and hung outside. They threw much needed light into the dark air, made worse by the sleety rain. It was also starting to blow hard.

He went to light a fire in the protected fire pit, which was right outside the stable, but again found that it was full of rubbish. He cleaned it out and lit a huge fire, large orange and yellow flames spitting out the dampness of the wood as it flared, bringing warmth and more light to the surrounding area.

A large pot filled with rainwater was hung above the fire, the cover keeping the blowing wind and rain out. The large pot should quickly warm, and he searched in the back of the stable for where he had stashed all the remnants of his father's remedies, finding the soothing salve, dried herbs and the very last bottle of bitters, which he knew must be at least 30 years old. The seal was not broken, however, and he knew that it should be fine. He had used these remedies before on Daisy and Dandy whenever they were sick, always trusting the natural way of healing, just like his father had taught him.

He suddenly thought of Dandy, Daisy's only, but beautiful colt, sadly sent away to a secret farm in England because they threatened to kill him, because Tom would not sell him to the gypsy clan, who he'd beaten hands down in a race.

"Oh God, Mam, what a bloody mess," he quietly cried as he worked laying out everything ready for Daisy.

"We are leaving, Tom!" said Keiron gingerly placing the house keys on the shelf inside the door, along with a large pot of hot tea, and a pile of sandwiches on a plate.

"Fuck off, Keiron, I'll sort you and Mary later," he replied.

"Oh, Tom we really are really, really, sorry!" he again cried out in alarm.

"Fuck off!" was all he had the strength to reply at that moment, disgust bringing bile to his throat at the realisation that some of his own family had hurt and mistreated this most honest and gentle beast. His own shame was also rising, he should have come sooner, he kept telling himself, but to no avail, it wouldn't do anyone any good to keep going over and over the past events, he had to deal with the here and now.

Sudden words kept entering his head, making him come out of his daydream of horror and sadness. Keiron retreated from the now sparkling clean stable to help Mary pack their car and then they left. Tom watched them go. He checked everything, took a long slug of tea, and ate one of the cheese and onion soda bread sandwiches. He realised that he was hungry; the last food he had consumed had been the previous night on the ferry, and that had just been sandwiches that Megan had made for him. Now his tummy was calling for more. He quickly bolted another down, satiating his hunger just for the moment, just enough to keep him going while he worked.

"Be Jesus, the silly cow still can't make soda bread," he murmured to himself as the last of it went down his throat. Depending on what he was going to find, he might not have another chance to eat and drink for hours, so he set about downing all of the remaining sandwiches and hot sweet tea. He then took a quick look around the now spotless stable and put his holdall to one side on top of a large bale of straw he had brought in to act as a table should he need it. The stable was now warm and well-lit, but the storm still rallied outside, building in strength. The fire in the fire pit burned brightly, but he fetched extra wood, just in case it was needed, and found Daisy's halter, still hanging on the nail exactly where he had left it 3 years ago when she had first come to live with Keiron and Mary.

He stopped for a moment to take a breath; his heart was pounding, fear running through his massive body almost seeping into his warm blood, rushing to his distressed brain. He had to steady himself. Saying out loud a prayer of protection and asking for help, he suddenly realised that he had a bottle of holy water in his pocket. He uncorked it and sprinkled it all around the stable, as well as outside, and over himself, chanting the exor chant as he went. When he was happy everything was in place, he picked the halter off the nail - it had the name DAISY sewn on it in multicoloured thread - and sprinkled it with the last of the holy water.

"Right, Lord," he said out loud, "time to go and find my girl!"

Chapter 26

Death – a new beginning

DAISY HAD MANAGED TO GET tight into a somewhat dry and sheltered corner of the hedges at the bottom of the field to try and get out of the storm. She had rested to her knees to try and protect her head which was so sore, and she was now fixed firmly into a little dry spot right at the bottom of a leafy hole in the hedge, totally protected from the raging cold and sleety rain and wind which hammered her soaking wet and battered body. Her head was sheltered just for the moment, with only a few gorse spikes, attacking her now throbbing and puss covered face.

She was in pain, everything hurt so bad and never before had she felt this way, and it was hard to even move. She was stuck and so thirsty but her tongue just would not work anymore. She was sure this was it; the end it just seemed like everything was dissolving into oblivion.

"I know Master Tom is coming to help me," she kept saying over and over again to herself, as she surely knew the arrow of death was pointing directly at her.

"Please, Daisy hold on, Master Tom is coming I promise," said the large gold and brown angel now stroking her face, singing to her to keep her awake, but she was fading fast. "Don't give up now!" he demanded of her, singing even louder and louder, trying so hard to keep her still lucid and awake in the growing storm which was raging around her.

TOM SET OUT WITH THE lamp, her halter and a long thick rope into the growling storm, tears of fear and shame dripping down his face, praying to find his girl alive, so he could help her pass peacefully, and not die unloved and untouched in a field, like so many had recently. He had asked Johnny to call Reagan to see if he could come around, as he might need him. His mind whirled just like the rain and sleet that surrounded him, misting his vision and the grey darkening skies made the search for Daisy even more difficult.

He started calling. "Daisy! Daisy!" looking all around trying to peer through the spiky rain that was falling but he could not see her. He decided to follow the hedge around the perimeter, as this is where animals would usually shelter from the weather, and he was sure she was near; he could sense her aura somewhere nearby. Again he called into the swirling rain and sleet which was biting his face, stinging him, making his eyes run, but still he pushed on, calling and calling; he had to find her.

Daisy suddenly thought she heard Master Tom. Was it a dream she asked herself, could it be the rain? Was she imagining it? Her mind was questioning the sudden sounds and constantly spinning. She was almost comatose with pain and cold, but again she heard the same voice calling to her. She tried whickering, but nothing would come out of her dry and crusty mouth.

"He's here, Daisy," said the angel to her gently, "he's come to take you home."

Oh, Master Tom please find me, she thought.

Tom suddenly sensed where she was just as he heard a call and saw a light from the yard at the house.

Oh thank God, Tom thought. "Reagan, down here!" he shouted loudly, hoping he could hear him through the storm and vigorously waving the lamp so he could see where he was in the field. As he turned the corner, where the two large hedges met, one a gorse the other a beech, Tom saw a body of a donkey. At first he thought she was dead but then he glimpsed movement. "Daisy! Daisy!" he called, bile rising in his throat at the sight of this dear beast, struggling for life. And struggling she was. She was down on her knees and stuck, but dear God in heaven, she was still alive. "Daisy girl," he wept, as he reached her and placed his hands on her ravaged body. She was skin and bones, sores pierced through all the skin on the back of her body, and when he gently pulled her head back from the little hidey hole she had found, he almost fainted with the sight that greeted him. One of her eyes had totally gone, burst with infection, the poison of the gorse doing its known evil, and the other wasn't far off. Her face was raw, the gorse reaping its vile revenge. "Oh Daisy girl, what have we all done to you?" he wept, as he rubbed her ears, and body, crying, trying to take his little friend's pain away.

"Oh, Master Tom, you have come, thank you, thank you," she said out loud in her mind, slowly closing the only eye she had left. She was relieved that she would not die alone in the corner of the field. "Don't cry, Master Tom, thank you for finding me, I'll be fine now the angels told me."

"Yes you will, Daisy," Tom replied to her, trying to reassure her.

"Tom!" came the call from Reagan, as he took in the scene before him before dropping to his knees beside his old friend in sheer shock at the sight of Daisy. "Oh dear God in heaven!" he said, as he looked at this once beautiful beast suffering and dying in front of his eyes, obviously in terrible pain. Tom was now vigorously rubbing her back and legs, trying to get some blood flowing around her decimated body. "I'll phone the Garda and get them to report the pair of them to the ISPCA," he said, tears now falling like rivulets, realising he too had let Daisy down. "Oh, God how could they do this?" the words stumbling slowly from his very ashamed and humbled mouth.

"Right then, Reagan, let's worry about that later, we have to get her up, and back to the stable, so let's concentrate on that shall we?" he said gently, trying to be calm around his dying friend. "Now, Reagan, we need to get this rope around her middle and help her up," he told him.

"She'll never get up, Tom; shall I go and get the bolt? I know how to use it since I had to put Arthur down, it'll be quick and painless, Tom," he mumbled, as the rain dribbled down his sorrowful face, still trying to accept the vision of this sadly abused beast in front of him.

"She'll get up, Reagan," he turned and told him firmly. "Now place the rope."

The two men worked quickly and quietly in the worsening storm, moving her body gently to place the thick rope around her middle, trying not to alarm Daisy. They continued rubbing her body and legs harder and harder to get blood flow which she would need to right herself.

"Right then, m'girl, I know you won't like this, but it should get you up, then we'll take you back to your stable, okay?" he told her gently.

"Yes, Master Tom," she replied meekly.

"My God, Tom, are you talking to Daisy?" Reagan asked dumfounded.

"You know, Reagan, I think I am," he replied, not even realising what he was saying, as he opened a little bottle of bitters that he took from his jacket pocket; it contained a secret formula his father always used when a horse was cast in his box. It was so bitter; it worked on the animal's senses, making it react violently, but in the right way, made the body jump up to attention. His father had also been a herbalist, and only ever treated horses and farm animals with natural remedies. It usually worked and by God it had better work tonight, as it was the only one he had. He had said a prayer when he found it in the back of the stable, thanking the Lord for being with him, because this just might save Daisy, well help her anyway. The saddest thing was he didn't have the recipe, because it had helped so many in the past.

He opened Daisy's sore and crusty mouth, which must have hurt her badly, and shook all the contents of the little bottle into her mouth. In about 5 seconds, the taste shot through her whole body like an electric shock, and she unbelievably jumped up onto her feet.

"God in heaven, in all my days, Tom, I've never seen anything like that, she was as good as dead!" Reagan commented.

"Well she's not dead so let's get this little lady to her stable, quick as we can."

"Righto," replied Reagan, as he held her steady.

The large rope tied around her waist enabled them to guide her slowly, and very lamely towards the stable through the bad light and nasty wind and rain that swirled around them as they made their way there, across the barren muddy field. Daisy was very lame and slipped a few times. Her shoes were long gone, and her hooves curled and unbalanced, which made the whole process of walking, uncomfortable and difficult, but the two men held her firmly, walking and talking to her to reassure her they were both there for her as they slowly padded their way towards the light of the warm and welcoming stable in the distance.

"Oh, Master Tom you found me, thank you," cried Daisy as she stumbled towards the lights in the distance, twice stopping to falter, but both men just held her firm making sure she was going forwards and not down. They would not allow her to fail, and supported her and pushed her on towards the lovely warm clean stable that was waiting for her.

I am safe now, I can just about see the stable through the storm, and the fire in the pit is burning brightly; that's the way home. Master Tom and Reagan are helping me. The pain is bad and I keep stumbling and at times Master Tom has to hold my head up. I feel so weak; I am so thirsty that my tongue feels like a dry stone in my mouth, and my eyes hurt. Oh, angels please help me make it to the stable, so I can die in peace. I know I am dying: I have never felt like this before, so if it is my time, then let me die gently, without pain, and take that last breath in the warm, with my master beside me. He'll make it right, I know he will, help me, angels, she called out in her mind as she stumbled towards warmth and safety, with two strong arms supporting her.

The stable was warm and welcoming, and the thick bed of straw felt so good to a very sick and cold animal that was on her last legs. Tom had already decided that he would stay with her tonight, as it would probably be her last, and he had to make her as comfortable as possible.

Reagan was distraught. He thought that he had seen cruelty in the past, but this was of a different magnitude. "Tom I'll go and get the Garda, they can report this to the ISPCA, and have those bastards brought up in court for this. It's a bloody outrage, that's what it is."

"Yes you do that, Reagan, thank you."

"Anything else I can do, Tom?" he asked through shocked, teary eyes.

"No thank you, Reagan, I'll settle her down now," he replied as he brought in the warm pot of water that was hanging in the fire pit.

Daisy lay on her side, the good eye blinking at the warm soft lights. Tom raised her head up at an angle, so she could see then he gently washed her broken body, salving all the sores, and cleaning out the pussy socket of her eye, closing it, after filling it with a mixture of warm cotton wool, herbs and salve to help the pain. He squeezed the juice of the warm apple which he still had in his pocket, and mixed it with a little honey he had brought as a present for Johnny's wife in his holdall, and some warm water, and trickled it into her mouth. Her tongue was solid and swollen, and most of the mixture trickled away down the side, but a little got through, releasing the stiff tongue and bringing liquid relief to a dehydrated and starving animal. All the while he worked, he calmly and quietly whistled an old Irish tune to keep her relaxed and free from worry.

Angels walked around the warm stable while he saw to her.

"Excuse me," said Tom, asking one to move as he gently tended her.

A soft donkey smile appeared on her face. The water honey and apple juice seemed to be working; she was peaceful, happy, knowing she was no longer alone, with someone actually now caring for her, and the constant whistling, and angel songs made her sleepy and slowly a warm feeling of safety and contentment spread through her painful body. She let out a large donkey sigh and Tom rubbed her tummy and smiled. It was a sad smile, but he knew now her passing wasn't far off, and she would be fine, he'd make sure of it.

Tom covered Daisy with a heavy large hessian blanket, it was hers, he had made it for her years ago when she had a bad cough and was poorly for a couple of weeks and she needed some extra warmth to get her through the cold nights. He settled down beside her in the thick straw, and placed her head in his lap, smoothing those once fluffy ears, singing to her, and remembering wonderful thoughts of his mother, the Sunday cart, Daisy in her hat at the wedding, and of course the race.

Reagan came into the stable, suddenly bringing him back to the now, making him realise just how tired and hungry he was. "Tom, this is Shamus O'Malley, he's the vet I was telling you about, I work with him. He'll examine Daisy and make the complaint to the Garda in the morning."

"Thank you, Shamus," replied Tom, not moving, but reaching out his hand in friendship and thanks.

"She's in a bad way, Tom," he told him, reacting badly to the sores and gashes on her body as he lifted the hessian blanket, and breathing in a sharp gasp of disgust as he examined the eye socket where one of her eyes should have been. "Must have been in agony for months, poor old beast. Tom, do you want me to put her down? I can do it now, save her having any more pain?" he asked quietly.

"No, Shamus, thank you, she'll pass on peacefully, I'll make sure of that," he replied.

"You do this?" Shamus asked him, looking at the salved and packed eye socket.

"Yes I did."

"Well, Tom, it's better than any vet would do, where did you learn the craft?"

"My father, Miles, God rest his soul," he replied quietly, not looking at him, still concentrating on Daisy who now appeared to be comfortable.

"Well, Tom, Miles certainly taught you well, and the trick with the bitters, amazing, it's a shame all the old remedies have been replaced in medicines now, some of them were the best," he told him as he made out a large pink criminal offence form, and signed it, giving it to Reagan, who had appeared with a large slice of cold apple pie and a large mug of hot sweet tea for Tom.

"Oh, Reagan, God bless you, friend."

"No, Tom, God bless you," he remarked, passing over the apple pie and tea.

"Well I don't think she'll make it till the morning, Tom, and if you need me, you know I will come back."

"Thank you, Shamus, but I can pass her on, it's the least I can do."

"Very well. Goodnight, Tom, it's been very humbling to meet you," and with that he left, leaving Tom and Reagan with Daisy, Reagan gripping the pink form in his hand, fisted in rage.

"I'll take this to the Garda now, Tom, there's a sergeant on night duty."

"Thank you, Reagan," Tom replied, passing back the empty mug, sweeping the pie crumbs from his shirt, and once again rubbing Daisy's ears, and whistling a soft Irish tune.

"Let's hope to God that this teaches everyone a lesson, Tom," said Reagan, as he started to leave the stable, just turning for one moment and whispering goodbye to Daisy, as he knew he would never see her alive again. The little rivulets of tears running down his face as he walked towards his van, were the only telltale sign of the love he would allow anyone to see that he had for that special once in a lifetime beast.

The storm raged outside, but the stable was warm and clean, and pain and tiredness took them both into oblivion, not knowing what the following frightening hours would bring.

Daisy woke suddenly, she was finding it hard to breathe and angels were gathered all around her as she now lay on the thick straw bed, her damaged head still in Master Tom's lap.

"Help me!" she called out to the angels in the stable.

"Don't panic, Daisy," said the large brown and gold angel, he was gently rubbing her nose and singing to her. Her tongue wouldn't move; it was stuck in her mouth like a large stone plugging her lungs just like a large rock would plug a hole in a dam. Panic was setting in, she was gasping, hardly able to take in any air and she felt paralysed. "Don't fight it, Daisy, just relax," he said, still rubbing her nose, as a big wet donkey tear tumbled down her cheek from the eye she could see with.

"I'm dying," she gasped, suddenly seeing the golden light emerge from the storm outside into the stable. Quietness was suddenly all around and Daisy found herself floating in a golden sea of light. All her pain had gone and she had taken her final breath. Stars sparkled all around her, dancing in formation in front of her eyes. Breathing was no longer a problem. All she could hear was the angels singing and all she could see was a soft light getting brighter and brighter; then darkness took her!

Tom woke, and Daisy's body shuddered violently, letting him know that she had just taken her last breath, and she was now with the angels. His wail and sobs were muffled by the driving storm outside. It wouldn't do any good now anyway he realised, she was gone. He prayed hard that she had passed painlessly. Her body was still warm, and he rubbed her ears with affection.

"Thank you, Daisy, for everything! For working hard, loving my children, and looking after Mam."

He cried alone in the stable, with just the broken body of a gentle beast in his arms for company and the soft golden light from the oil lamps which still burned, giving comfort and some warmth to this lonely place. Sleep would once again take this shattered man. Pain and worry had been in his life since he met and married his beloved wife Patsy, but this donkey had given him the strength to leave Ireland, always knowing she was looking after his ailing mother. It was his turn to thank her in the only way he knew, by being there with her at the end. He decided to stay in the stable with her body and would bury her in the morning, when the storm had passed. He got up and covered her with her blanket, and placed a single kiss on her forehead. He made a bed up just opposite her, and settled down to sleep, thoughts and worries again flooding into his head, but Daisy had passed, and he was with her. It felt like a knife had ripped his guts out.

"How much more pain and anguish will I have to take?" he constantly asked himself, but the angels surrounded him, and sleep came quickly, and deeply to a tired and tormented man.

***

"DAISY! DAISY!" CAME THE CALL into the stable. Daisy suddenly woke, lifted her head off of the thick straw floor, and looked outside. It was a beautiful sunlit morning, rays of soft golden light were streaming into the stable, and the air smelled crisp and clean.

"Mistress, is that you, Mistress?" Daisy called back, looking out of the opened stable door, and staring into the field which was lush with wild flower, tall grasses and brightly coloured flying insects of all shapes and sizes.

"Come on, lazy bones, we've work to do!" came the call from the little lady stood at the gate to the field with a halter in her hands.

"Coming, Mistress!" Daisy excitedly called back, getting to her feet; she felt well, her feet were beautifully shod with brand new shiny shoes, and she did a little dance on the spot with excitement.

"Don't look back now," called Margaret, whose heart was filled with pride and excitement at seeing Daisy coming to join her. "Well, lass, we're together again you and me. Ready to work?"

"Ready, Mistress," replied Daisy as Margaret put her halter on and gave her a big hug all around her neck, looking over towards the stable where her son lay asleep on the thick bed of straw he had made earlier.

"Angels," called Margaret to the gathering outside the stable door, "I need to see Tom my son, can you help me please?" she asked bowing with respect as Daisy stood beside her. The storm had started to die down and the temperature was rising; it would be a lovely day. "Please! I need to tell him something, something I should have told him years ago." The angels nodded, and turned to walk away.

Tom was suddenly woken; the banging of the stable door had brought him back into the real world once again. He looked over to the body of his dear friend, closed his eyes and said a little prayer.

"Tom! Tom Murphy!" came the voice of his mother Margaret.

Tom suddenly jumped up. "What in blazes! Is that you, Mam?" he called out, now turning to the opened stable door, and seeing in the distance, through the beautiful golden light, Daisy and his mother standing at the gate.

"Tom!" she again called.

He slapped his own face hard, and rubbed his eyes. "Mam, Daisy is that really you?" he called, not really believing his eyes.

"That it is, son. I need to tell you something, something I should have told you years ago, but I was too afraid."

"Oh, Mam, what is it?" he called back, half afraid of what he might hear.

"It's you, son, it's always been you!"

"What has, Mam?"

"You, son, you have the gift, really good, just like your father, Miles and his father before him, that's why you were chosen to look after Patsy."

"Oh, Mam, God in heaven, what are you saying?" he called back.

"You will make it through, son. It's going to be tough, but you'll beat the demon, well and truly, you will beat him, it's written. But Megan and Trixie are both heavily gifted, you will have to look after them, promise me, Tom."

"Oh God, Mam, what will I do?" he asked back, panicking now as they both started to turn and walk away.

Margaret stopped, turned and looked back at her beautiful son. "You'll know what to do, son, ask the angels for help, they've always been with you, and they will tell you what you need to do. It's just that they have been waiting to speak with you for a long time, now it's your turn, ask and listen."

"Oh God, Mam, I will, I will."

"Bye, son, love you!" she called, and Daisy whickered and did her little dance on the spot.

"Bye, Mam, bye, Daisy," he called, falling to his knees in sheer shock of the news he had just received, but now realising that absolutely everything was starting to make sense and fall into place. He stood up and put his hand over his eyes, squinting into the beautiful gold and silver rays piercing his vision, tears tumbling as he watched his mother and Daisy walk into the light in the distance. His mother's arm was raised, waving goodbye and Daisy was at her side, a small troupe of angels following them: mother and her companion back together again in death, but both now facing a new challenge and life together on the other side.

Thank God Daisy is with her, he thought, relieved that his mother was not alone, as he watched the light fade. Tom was still reeling with the previous night's events.

"Are you ready to start your work sorting out this demon inside Patsy, Tom?" asked the massive midnight velvet blue and gold angel stood at his side.

Tom turned, bowed and looked up into the beautiful golden eyes of the angel stood next to him. "Yes, yes I think I am now," he replied.

"Good! We have lots of work to do. Let's get Daisy's body sorted, and you home to England!"

"Yes, good Idea," replied Tom, now smiling, suddenly realising for the first time in years, he was not alone and that he had help. In fact it had been there all along, he just didn't realise it!

Epilogue

KEIRON AND MARY O'DONNELL WERE indeed hauled up before the Justices of the District Court in New Ross by the ISPCA and fined a massive, and never known before amount, of one hundred pounds, and found guilty of gross cruelty and neglect of an animal, and also of causing unnecessary suffering and death. They were banned from ever keeping another animal, including chickens. The ISPCA made sure their case made the headlines in the national papers, giving a stark and very firm warning that cruelty would not be tolerated, and further cases would be brought against anyone who dared to mistreat their animals. A new phone line was introduced so that people could anonymously report any wrongdoings, and as of that day, the cast was set.

In the meantime Keiron and Mary took the full wrath of the shocked community, so much so that they sold the house at a knock down price to Aiden McConnor, one of Tom's nephews, much to his pleasure, and fled, leaving the town in haste, full of shame and remorse for their terrible actions. No one knows where they are now, or even if they are still in Ireland, or if they are even alive. Nobody, not even their family let alone the outraged villagers, would ever worry or think about those nasty, cruel bastards ever again. Good riddance, crowds shouted as they saw their lorry, with all their belongings, leave the little town, both Keiron and Mary hiding their faces as the lorry pushed past.

Daisy was buried under the apple tree at the edge of the field, just by the gate where she had spent her last lonely years. Tom made sure her head collar was securely attached to his mother's headstone in the graveyard; it gave him some comfort knowing they were finally together again.

Reagan settled down into married life and very soon had a daughter who joined his newly adopted son, who he was now teaching to take over his business when he retired, just like his father had done for him.

Dandy was whisked away from Ireland for his own safety when the gypsies came looking for revenge. After finding out the reason why no other horse in Ireland could beat him, and ended up in a lovely riding centre for the disabled in Devon, where he became the centre of attention, and loved every minute, never knowing how near to death he was (and that's another tale).

Tom returned to England. Patsy was still very ill and the doctors were now very concerned, thinking they may have to operate on her brain. It was a terrible worrying time, but Tom was stronger now, he had the faith. His eyes had been opened by his mother, and he now accepted. He constantly said prayers of protection for his family and thanked the Lord up above for the final contact with his mother and Daisy that day through the ether.

And what of Margaret and Daisy I hear you all ask? Well, some say that on a warm summer's night as the sun is fading on the horizon, throwing long shadows across the fields, a little old lady and a donkey can be seen standing at the gate, just gazing over the field into the dying light, suddenly disappearing when the light fades. I don't know for sure, but the locals do; the legend of Daisy the donkey will never die!

Printed in Great Britain
by Amazon